Not Anyone's Wife

A Zimbell House Anthology

Not Anyone's Wife

A Zimbell House Anthology

ZIMBELL HOUSE PUBLISHING

UNION LAKE, MICHIGAN

© 2018 Zimbell House Publishing

Published in the United States by Zimbell House Publishing
http://www.ZimbellHousePublishing.com
All Rights Reserved

Trade Paper ISBN: 978-1-947210-63-9
Kindle ISBN: 978-1-947210-64-6
Digital ISBN: 978-1-947210-65-3
Library of Congress Control Number: 2018908999

First Edition: September 2018
10 9 8 7 6 5 4 3 2 1

ZIMBELL HOUSE PUBLISHING
UNION LAKE

Acknowledgments

Zimbell House Publishing would like to thank all those that contributed to this anthology. We chose to showcase four new voices that best represented our vision for this work.

We would also like to thank our Zimbell House team for all their hard work and dedication to these projects.

Contents

A Radio-Ready Romance ... 1

Matt McGee

Expired Sicilian ... 41

Joanna Bair

The Fly Girl ... 59

E. W. Farnsworth

The Wives Discuss … ... 77

Alana Ballantyne

Contributors ... 95

Similar Anthologies from Zimbell House ... 101

Coming Soon from Zimbell House ... 103

A Note from the Publisher ... 105

A Radio-Ready Romance

Matt McGee

Lives Apart

Before they even knew each other, Nate and Cathi were addicted to their radios. She liked The Baby Snooks Show, not so much because she liked the idea of a little girl blathering away in a high voice, but the fact that she always put the adults in their place—especially that know it all father of hers. It gave Cathi a secret thrill; she'd read plenty about Fanny Brice's story, her years in the Ziegfeld Follies. Cathi suspected that the lady named after a part of the human anatomy was more likely to kick a man right in his posterior than shake hers in the hope of getting a mate to set her up in a house with a couple kids. Those kids, she was sure, would drown out the radio show she loved so much.

And screw that, she thought.

But her real love, of course, was for Eve Arden of Our Miss Brooks. A strong female lead, Arden was a teacher at a high school where she dealt with the daily headaches of her ever-pubescent co-stars, a bellowing principal, but most of all—Miss Brooks was always trying to get the clueless, and single, Mr. Boyington to stop paying attention to his experiments long enough to think about performing a few experiments with her. Cathi loved Arden's strength, and though she wouldn't admit it out loud, it made her feel less alone in her day to day life.

Hooking a man wasn't Cathi's first priority. Sure, she wasn't opposed to the idea of having a friend around to make the nights less lonely, but that would have to happen on her own terms. In the meantime, she'd just go out to the grocery store, buy some Lustre Cream Shampoo—Brooks' sponsor—and a box of Post Toasties as advertised on Fanny's show and go home, crawl in bed with a good book and be well rested for work the next day.

Nate, on the other hand, was the Great Gildersleeve type. He tuned in every Sunday to the exploits of the most eligible bachelor in the fictional town of Summerfield and revel in the man's self-determination. That's for me, he thought, raising a family he'd inherited rather than reared himself, living life in an office of his own downtown, a parlor at home where he could relax, smoke a cigar, and have Birdie, the maid, at his beck and call. Yep, that sounded pretty good, although truth be told, he was secretly embarrassed by the way Birdie was treated in each week's show, like an idiot servant with one catch-phrase. Sure, the studio audience applauded on cue, but Nate suspected that listeners like himself felt demeaned along with Birdie. He decided to do her a little justice in the only way he knew how, by using her name in his company's title.

Nonetheless, Nate tuned in every Sunday. Each week, usually Tuesdays when he did his shopping, he'd buy whatever he'd heard advertised by Kraft on Gildersleeve. He'd take it home and squirrel it away. He didn't really like macaroni and cheese from a box, but each purchase felt like bringing a little piece of Summerfield into his modest, Craftsman-style home.

Neither Nate nor the female neighbor he'd yet to meet would admit it, but the radio was a perfect soundtrack of white noise to their lives. With radio, there was a voice where there often were no voices. The radio gave a sense in their living room that there was a human presence when, at least for the moment, there would otherwise be silence.

Shopping Day

Nate and Cathi met in the most basic, modern way; they bumped into each other at the grocery store. It was a Saturday night, for neither of them their regular shopping day, but both had run out of something that needed buying right away. Nate had already grabbed his obligatory slab of Kraft Velveeta and was standing in the snack aisle, trying to make sense of the Jolly Time popcorn. "How do you cook this stuff?" he mumbled as he took a step back to do a bit of thinking and, as he took that step, there was Cathi, pushing her yet-to-be-filled cart down the snack aisle.

He bumped right into her.

"Oh, excuse me," he volunteered immediately, "I'm sorry about that."

"It's okay, I wasn't really looking where I was going either."

Cathi smiled at this last line since it was basically true. She'd been looking, but mostly at the rope-like shape of Nate's forearm. He'd worn his shirtsleeves rolled up, not normal for a man of 1940s, and what a delightful turn when he started to back up; she actually thrust out a hip to deflect him. *Deflect … is that what you call doing the cha-cha into someone who doesn't see you coming?*

She decided it was a good time to shop for snacks.

Nate kept trying to make sense of his selection. He picked up one jar, then another, as if one would have a different set of more sensible directions. She looked at the popcorn, kinda, but kept sneaking little looks his way. She pulled a bag of potato chips down and studied the bag.

"Can't go wrong with the classics," he said.

Cathi was delightfully startled at his voice. "Are potato chips considered a classic now?"

"Potato chips got me through my childhood. It was the go-to whenever someone was gonna come over to play in the backyard."

Cathi nodded like she understood then she said, "Well, I guess if I buy the chips, then all I need is someone to come over and play in the yard."

She heard herself say these words, felt the sly grin stretch across her face, pleased that her inner Miss Brooks was bubbling to the surface at just the right moment.

Nate pretended to be reading the popcorn label. "I guess that depends. Do you have a swing set?"

The sly grin turned into a thoughtful smile. It crawled over her face. It sounded like fun, being with this man.

"I've got a porch swing," she said. "Will that do?"

"I love a good swing on a lovely evening."

Cathi's heart suddenly leapt into her throat, no doubt a remnant from her years with those awful nuns she'd put up with in elementary school. It was like they'd installed some kind of kind of birth control to block words like the ones she was about to say from coming up. But she overcame it, and apparently, just in time.

"482 Evergreen Terrace," she said.

Nate nodded. "Eight o'clock?"

Cathi nodded.

Nate held up the jar. "I'll bring the popcorn."

She held up her chip bag. "Leave it home. Bring something to drink instead."

Nate smiled and looked her in the eye, "What goes with potato chips?"

"Bourbon."

Nate dropped the jar into his cart and looked down the aisle. "I better finish my shopping. Store's about to close, and I still need a lot of things from the pharmacy."

Cathi felt a sudden urge of concern, sympathetically she responded, "Oh, is someone ill?"

Nate smiled over his shoulder as he went. "No. Just party favors."

Had he been closer, Cathi might've smacked him. *Arrogant bastard. Just because a woman invites you for a swing on her porch doesn't mean she wants to swing anywhere else.*

Then again, who was she kidding? She wouldn't mind an hour or so of swinging. *Isn't that what Stanwyck was doing in that movie I'd seen? What was the name of it? Doesn't matter.* Besides, she'd heard Stanwyck wasn't interested in men. *God bless her heart,* Cathi thought. *Not my cup of tea but good for her, doing what she wants and not being ashamed.*

Cathi had a little Stanwyck in her. Fearlessness. The ability to tell someone what was on her mind and not back off. After all, she'd just done it right there with that guy. *Ah damn, what was his name?* She realized he'd never given it. And she'd never given hers. Suddenly something felt as if it needed to be finished. She looked up for him, but he was gone.

She'd just have to wait until six-thirty to find out.

The Long Walk Home

Cathi could take a bus from her house to the store, and for only a dime. On this particular Sunday though, she got off a half-mile before her neighborhood. She had a bag of groceries to consider, but there was nothing that would rot right away. Besides, she had to check in on her investment.

Eight years earlier, Cathi had come into what people often referred to as 'a little bit of money.' In her case, that little bit was $43,000. She bought her home outright, invested most of the remainder so she could be comfortable, and began a slow, unhurried search for a reasonable investment, something that might bring her daily happiness and a sense of worth.

That investment, made against her families better advisement, was a malt shop. Originally called Pop's, the Depression had been too much for ol' Pop, and it had been boarded up in 1940 after the owner decided he couldn't make a go of it anymore.

When the inheritance came through in '41, Cathi had been riding the bus back and forth to the store one afternoon, thinking about the shows that would be on that evening. It was a Sunday, and that meant only one thing—Jack Benny. Then there would be that Gildersleeve show and a good new detective show she'd discovered. She was thinking about all this, how she'd double-check the times in Radio Mirror, when the bus rolled past Pop's boarded up shop.

Like a strike of lightning, she knew this was it. The following week she made a deal, signed the papers and two weeks later, found herself knee-deep in the burger business. She bought herself a new apron, spatula, and turned the 'CLOSED' sign around and opened for business on a Monday.

It wasn't but six hours into that first day when Cathi realized there was a crucial missing link in the whole plan. Sure, any idiot could flip a burger and draw an ice cream soda for a guy and his gal, crack a few jokes and collect their twenty cents. But there was something else missing, and Cathi realized immediately what it was.

There were suppliers to find and workers to deal with. There was the bread delivery man, the guy shipping in all those phosphates, the deep freeze that kept the ice cream frozen and went on the blink twice a week. All these things piled up, one right after another, and Cathi soon realized she'd have to take care of them and put her cooking aside. She hired Pop to come back and take over the grille.

"You'd be the perfect face on the place once again. People like you. And you wouldn't have to deal with all the little things. The purchasers, the maintenance. The headaches. That would be my thing now."

"Not women's work," Pop said.

"Let me decide what is and isn't women's work. Meanwhile, you be the pretty face on Pop's. Alright, Pop?"

The older man seemed to hesitate.

"How 'bout it Pop? We got a deal?"

Pop finally smiled and said, "Yeah. We can work this out."

Cathi learned quickly that she was good at this stuff. She could not only keep a business, but she also had a head for it. The following year Pop's was not only making money, but she was also able to pay Pop himself more than he'd been making back when he was his own boss. He certainly had fewer headaches. Like she'd promised, all he had to do was show up and be pretty.

Cathi had found something she was truly good at. Not having been a mother, running Pop's seemed the closest she'd get to raising and maintaining a living thing.

After she'd left the grocery store that day, running the episode with Nate back through her mind, she got off the bus a half mile early.

Pop's was bustling. Summertime meant bored high school kids with pocket change. Even a few of their younger siblings were there, though the younger ones were made to stay on the sidewalk, out of their older sibling's hair. Cathi had followed Pop's suggestion, and in April she secured a secondhand jukebox. That put them over the top; young faces and even a few hep adults became regulars. Pop's was, once again, the place to be.

Cathi turned her back on the front door to protect the grocery bag and pushed it open with her backside.

Across the room she set her groceries under the counter, beside the deep freeze where the ambient chill would do them good. Seeing the crowd, she tied on an apron.

"Hey Pops, business is pretty good, eh?"

"See for yourself. It's hopping, alright. You don't need to do that," he nodded toward the apron.

"I want to. Hey guys!" Cathi approached a table of regulars and swept away an armload of dirty dishes, float glasses, a few finished sodas. She made small talk as she did it then disappeared into the back room. Four passes of the main room and she had a full sink.

In the backroom, she reached up for the Rinso flakes—sponsor of Amos & Andy, she'd often talk to herself in her best Kingfish voice while she scrubbed. Cathi swirled the whole basin with her arm, created the sudsy lather she wanted and started rinsing with the sprayer. Once the food bits were off, she dropped glasses and plates into the swirl and got to washing.

"Ain't you gonna bother with gloves?" Pop said through the order window.

"Why? I'm not vain."

Pop shook his head. "Maybe that's because there ain't no man back at your house to impress. But I'll give you this. Can't say as I know a lot of business owners who drop in just to wash dishes in their off-time."

"I'm telling you, I wanna do it Pops. Takes a little heat off you, and it gives me a break from counting my millions."

"Right. Lady's making millions selling ten cent hamburgers and I'm a monkey's uncle."

Cathi dried her hands. "Say hello to your Uncle Bonzo for me," she smiled.

Soon she carried a rack of refreshed glasses and stoneware out the swinging double doors and set it on the prep counter. She put plates in their proper stacks and reloaded Pop's stock of soda glasses. Business had calmed down. Some of the kids had gone off to do other things around town. The jukebox hadn't played in almost twenty minutes. Soon, Cathi and Pop had the place to themselves.

"Usually gets slow this time of day," he said. "Kids realize the new lifeguard has come on duty at the pool. Girls say he's a real dreamboat."

"So where are the boys?"

"Keeping an eye on the girls."

Cathi smiled. "Aw c'mon. Are kids really still that way?"

"Jealousy is as old as the hills my dear."

"Well," Cathi said, "give me a man who's just happy letting me go my way and I'll let him go his."

Pop rubbed his hands clean on a towel. "They have a name for that you know."

"Happiness?" she guessed.

"Spinsterhood."

Cathi watched Pop throw the towel in the dirty linen, turn and disappear into the backroom.

"Sounds pretty good to me," she said.

She'd sit and talk to Pop almost another hour, then the dinner rush began. "Folks on their way to the movies," he said. "It's part of a night out on the town.

We give 'em what they want fairly quick. Drops right off, and right before the eight o'clock picture."

Cathi held up a single finger. "Speaking of eight o'clock, don't let me stay too long."

"Going to the picture show?"

Cathi let a few visuals jump around in her head.

"What was that," Pop smiled.

"What?"

"You just grinned. What are you up to?"

"Just … I'm meeting someone, that's all."

"Ah. A rendezvous." Pop looked toward the window wistfully. "I remember those."

"You can still go out on dates Pop. Why don't you?"

"Are you kidding? Who would I date in this town? Besides, boss lady's got me slaving away …"

Cathi held up her hands, surrendering. "Okay, I can take a hint. Hand me my groceries."

Pop leaned down to the cubby where she'd stashed the bag hours earlier. He'd just lifted it when the bell on the door rang.

The man who walked in didn't remove his hat. He was young, but on the edge of losing that as well. His suit said he had money somewhere, but his stride said he had all the time in the world to think about which sucker was going to be scammed out of a twenty-dollar bill next. To Cathi, he bore more than a passing resemblance to Richard Widmark.

He looked Pop's way. "You the owner?"

Pop hooked a thumb at the lady at the counter. The one with the grocery bag and the look of having just bussed tables. The guy sized her up. He took a toothpick and punched it into his teeth.

"You, sister?"

Cathi leaned both elbows on the counter behind her and stared him down. "Me. And since I know my family history I know you ain't my brother, so speak your piece and shove off, *brother*."

The guy slid sideways onto a counter stool. "Wow. Quite a feisty one, aren't you?"

"I don't do feisty. You need something to eat?"

"Nope."

"Drink?"

"Strike two."

"News flash Mystery Man, I don't play ball. Not with cheap hoods or smart boys."

The guy reached toward his breast pocket. From the corner of her eye, Cathi saw Pop move into position, ready for whatever might come out. Cathi gave the slightest shake of her head. Pop backed off, but not far.

The guy pulled out a business card. With the grace of a smoker, he handed the introduction over to Cathi. She read.

"See this Pop? Says he's Paul Leonard."

"My friends call me Leo."

"Hear that Pop, his friends call him Leo. Maybe his friends can't spell his whole last name. Says here he's a supplier. Birdie's Bread Company. We got enough bread Pop?"

"Lousy with it. In fact, I'd say there are some kinds we can do without."

"Certainly the kind old Paul Leo-Nard here is selling."

"Hey look," the guy tried to rationalize. "I'm just a seller."

"Yeah? We ain't buying." Cathi snapped the card so it carried halfway across the room. "Hit the bricks, smart boy. And pick up that trash while you're on your way out."

Paul gave her a stare, then went over, bent down, picked the card up and returned it to his breast pocket.

"Some friends of mine might not be happy we didn't get better acquainted."

"Yeah?" Cathi didn't blink. "Some friends of mine would be awful glad to know that some know-nothing thug was trying to move in on their route. I'll be sure and let my friends know that you dropped in, Mr. … What was your name again?"

"Leonard," Pops said.

The guy shook his head. "Some people," he said. "You try to come in and talk business."

"Yeah, nice talking to you. Don't get lost on your way out of town."

A few steps, then the door closed behind Paul Leonard.

Cathi waited through almost ten seconds of silence. "You know him, Pops?"

"Never seen him."

"Let me know if he comes back."

"He won't."

"You heard the man. Instead of backing up his threats he walked out of here. That's not a big boy with connections, he's a child with memories of having been a bully."

Pop leaned against the counter to shift the weight off his feet. "I gotta' hand it to ya, Cathi. Not a lot of dames I know can handle a business, much less stare down a guy like that."

Cathi waved a limp hand. "I've been staring down guys like that since I was on the playground. You know what?"

"Hmm."

"They never change. All talk."

Pop studied his knuckles. "Speaking of talk, what was this you were saying before about a rendezvous?"

Cathi shot up straight. "Oh damn. What time is it?"

Pop looked at his watch. "Quarter til eight."

"Damn! Hand me my groceries Pop."

Pop lifted the bag. His forearms flexed impressively as he performed the light duty; oftentimes, before she'd taken over the shop, his arms had waddled with proof that he didn't mind sampling his own cooking.

"Thanks," Cathi said. She grabbed the bag and skittered toward the door. "Call the house if there are any emergencies."

Pop leaned a bored elbow on the counter. "There won't be."

Cathi gripped the doorknob.

"Good. Then consider the do not disturb sign out," she grinned.

Swing Date

There were no buses this time of night, so Cathi had to skitter her way home. She used one hand to hold her hat in place, the other arm she kept wrapped around her groceries. She could practically tabulate the cost of shoe leather, grinding away beneath her feet in little shavings as her soles met the cement walk. The city had designed the walks so that they were rough, had a certain amount of grip when needed during the winter, when snow and ice tried to stick. It was smart, but the rest of the year it just wore your shoes down and put you in the shoemaker's repair shop that much sooner.

Cathi came within twenty feet of her house. There he was, back to her, relaxed on the porch swing. His hat was off. Judging by the trim line along his neck, he'd been shaved and had a haircut. He'd put on a light coat, powder blue, wore the same white shirt, its cuffs buttoned now. *Damn.* The felt hat in his lap couldn't be but a couple months old. She smiled as she came into sight.

"Well," she said, coming up the sidewalk. "I hope I didn't keep you waiting long."

"Not at all. I was a little early. I like to be a little early wherever I'm going. Being late makes a bad impression."

"Yes, it does. You made quite a good one this afternoon."

"Aw shucks. I'm just a guy who likes a woman who knows her snack foods."

Cathi smiled. She sat beside him. "You left out one little detail."

"What's that?"

Cathi smiled. "Your name."

"Oh. Yes, I did. I'm Nate. Nate Dingle."

Cathi laughed.

"What?"

"Like the postman!"

Nate wasn't sure what was still so funny. "Your postman's name is Dingle?"

"No! You don't know the Daydreaming Postman?"

Nate shook his head lightly.

"Well," Cathi explained, "on The Baby Snooks show, there's this character who's a postman—"

"Oh, that postman."

"Right. And he's always daydreaming of other places he could be, you know. Other professions he might be doing instead. He's hilarious."

Nate sat back down on the swing. Cathi set her groceries aside and joined him. "Is that your favorite show? Fanny Brice?"

"Oh yes, Mr. Dingle," she giggled despite herself. "Sorry, I just love your last name."

"Don't wear it out."

"I won't," she smiled, and for the briefest moment, she let the words float through her head, *maybe I'll just try it on for a while and see how it fits.*

"How about you," she turned their conversation. "Favorite show?"

"Oh, that's easy. It used to be Fibber McGee, which is still really funny, but I have to confess … I love the Gildersleeve show."

"The big blowhard?"

"You say it like it's a fault."

"No. It's just, well …"

Nate waited. While Cathi thought, she stood up. She picked up the grocery bag and opened the unlocked front door. With a nod, they went inside. Nate left the door open and closed the screen.

"It's just what," he followed to the kitchen.

"It's just that … okay, take for instance his love interest. What's her name? Layla?"

"Leila."

"Right," Cathi said, "the southern belle woman. Well, now mind you I've listened to the show. And my take on Leila's character is that – and this is the writer's fault – that Leila is a conniving schemer just trying to manipulate the big man into giving her whatever her little heart desires. And then 'ohhh, Throckmorton!'" Cathi crooned in a southern drawl. "Why I'm ever so grateful to you for helping me clean out my dirty ol' coal bin. Why, I just haven't any idea about … 'man's work.'"

Nate waited.

"Then she's scheming to get him to reroof the porch or some damn thing. It presents women as weak to the point of having to trick a man into wanting to do their heavy lifting."

Cathi began unpacking the groceries. She took the Post Toasties out so she could put them in the pantry. She handed a bunch of celery to Nate, who instinctively put it in the icebox.

"Well," he said, "what of it?"

She put away the Toasties then handed him a bottle of milk to put it in the icebox.

"Well, it's just a little stereotypical, that's all." She handed him a dozen eggs, and while he put them away, she slipped her personal effects—soap, toothpaste, and shampoo—quickly back into the bag to be carried into the bathroom.

"Stereotypical," he repeated. "Okay, let me ask you something."

"Alright."

"Do you have many girlfriends?"

"A few."

"Do they, or any of the women you know act, well, helpless in order to get a man to do their work for them."

"Yep."

Nate held up his hands. "There ya go."

"But," Cathi said, "just because they act that way doesn't mean that a show that reaches millions every week should portray women in that light. In fact, that kind of stereotype only reinforces that kind of bad behavior, don't you think?" She handed him a second bottle of milk.

Nate put the bottle in the icebox. "Actually, it works the other way, wouldn't you say?"

"How so."

"Okay. Something personal about me. My father remarried. And when I hear a character like Leila Ransom croon in Gildersleeve's ear every week, I hear Dad's new wife, who has got him completely henpecked. I hear her about to manipulate him, and as an audience member I think 'oh boy Gildersleeve, look out bud.' If anything, hearing the hero getting hoodwinked by a woman with ill intent conditions us to see that kind of manipulation coming down the road … and to avoid it."

She handed him the butter. He turned to put it away when he caught her stare. She looked at him, then at the butter, and he caught on.

"Aw c'mon that's different."

"How."

"Well, first of all, I just want to be helpful. We're working as a team here, I'm not doing the heavy lifting while you go out to have a manicure."

"That's fair."

"And it's not like you're asking me to spend the afternoon fixing your car. Until you pointed it out, I just felt like we were doing this together. And third … well …"

"Well, what."

Nate was going to say something. Then he felt the bulge in his jacket pocket. As if on cue, he watched

Cathi pull out a single glass bottle of Coke she'd pilfered from the shop.

"Were you going to say 'because I like you.'"

"What if I was?"

She took the bottle and pushed it against his chest. It was a nice chest. "I'd say, first go mix us up a couple of drinks sailor. Then we can talk about the future. I assume you brought something to go with our snack."

Nate opened the top of the icebox, found the ice pick and chipped off enough for two drinks. He scooped the chips into a couple of glasses and found a bottle opener for the Coke. In fact, he found it right out in the open on top of the counter where she'd set it out for him.

"Make mine a little on the light side," she said. "Can't have me drunk in the early evening."

"I thought that was the best time to have a little load on?"

She sipped her bourbon and Coke. He'd made it perfect. Truly perfect. She lifted the glass in a toast. "Mmm. Well done. I'll have to have you over for all my parties."

"I'm not much of an entertainer."

"Oh, I bet you've got some song in your heart somewhere. But aside from bartending, how are you on the other side of the bar?"

"Don't spend much time there either," he said. "If an associate or a friend wants to meet for a drink, talk business, sure. But otherwise, it's not my first thought."

Good, she thought, *drinks but not a lush. Now for the big question.*

"So, Mr. Dingle, I'm going to guess by the lack of a tan line on your finger that you're not married."

"Nope. I was close once, but … didn't work out. How about you?"

Cathi sipped her drink and waved him toward the living room. "I'm nobody's wife. Never have been. I don't foresee myself getting hitched up. Frankly, I prefer being married to my work. When something breaks, I can fix it. When I feel like pitching in, I go down and roll up my sleeves and do it. Mostly, I just leave things to my associate."

"Sounds good to me. Oh, hey! We almost forgot." He darted back to the kitchen and returned with her chips. He'd taken his jacket off and draped it on the arm of a chair; when he returned with the bag, his sleeve was rolled up. The way he carried it, you'd think he was lifting weights. Cathi watched his forearm flex from out the end of his dress shirt again. She couldn't help watching the rope-like muscle as he waved the bag around.

"In the meantime, let's just lay back and enjoy some snacks."

"Right. I'm always up for sex … snacks! Snacks. Oh, my God, I meant snacks. Oh no …"

Nate loved seeing her blush. Perhaps feeling a need to save her from her own embarrassment, he handed her the bag. "Well, I'm sure you taste great too," he smiled. "But for right now, maybe we should just take it slow and start with chips."

She used the bag to partly cover her face. "I'm really good at opening these." She pulled both sides of the bag. It didn't open. She tried again. Still nothing. Nate reached over and took the bag from her hands.

"Don't be embarrassed. I'm sure as we get to know each other, I'll say a whole bunch of stupid stuff."

"Could you start now?"

Nate tore the bag easily and handed it back to Cathi. He looked at the ceiling, searching for a story to recite.

"When I met the woman I almost married," he began, "we were in high school. We were going up a stairwell, and I was the athletic type so I'd practically hop the stairs two at a time. She was the clumsy type, you know, the adorably goofy kind who can't keep her feet under her most of the time. Well, she slipped just as I was launching up two steps and boom, her heel kicked me right where you shouldn't kick a man."

Cathi took a chip and crunched it, staring at him as if he were a movie star, performing just for her. "And that's how you met?"

"Why not? It seemed as good a start as any. We already had the embarrassing stuff out of the way."

"Not all of it apparently." Cathi lifted her drink from the end table.

"How's that."

"Well, you said it didn't work out. Something must have derailed it."

Nate nodded in thought. "My grandmother used to have this favorite saying. She passed it along to my father, who would often say it to me. 'You two will be alright so long as you both keep rowing in the same direction.'"

"Your grandmother sounds like my kinda lady. So how did that apply?"

"It took a year or so, but I eventually found out we weren't both rowing in the same direction."

Cathi sifted through the bag for a good-sized chip. She handed it to Nate, who took it, said thanks. Then she fished out one for herself. "How so?"

"Well, let's just say I was a Gildersleeve fan, and she was more a disciple of Barbara Stanwyck."

"How uncanny," she said, "I was just thinking about her today. So are you saying your ex was a 'lady's best friend'?"

"I guess that's one way of saying it. And that's fine, you know. Better I found out when I did. Apparently, these feelings had been cooped up for some time. Something about our being together just brought it to the surface."

"Anything in particular?"

"You mean, do I think my manhood had been insulted?"

"I guess that's one way of saying it," she echoed. She sipped her bourbon and waited.

"No," he smiled. He shook the ice in his glass. "In retrospect, I'd have been far more insulted if I'd found out later, or been forced to live in a sham marriage."

"Or," she found another chip to wave like a wand, "if you had found her in bed with another woman."

Nate smiled. "I suppose this is where I'm supposed to say 'wow, a chance at a threesome.' Nah, I didn't want to share the person I loved."

Cathi swished her drink. She stayed mute.

"So enough about me. How about you? Any near misses in your past?"

"Ehh," she wavered, "I've had men interested, some were good men. But none seemed worth giving up the ability to determine my own destiny every day."

"I understand that. It isn't that I wouldn't love to have someone in my daily life. It's just that I can't see myself changing my day to day routines to accommodate someone else's whims and whines."

Cathi held up her glass in a toast. He got out of his chair, walked over, clinked his glass into hers, and they sipped. He stood appraisingly. Cathi stared at her glass.

"We're going to die alone, aren't we?"

Nate laughed. "It's way, way too early to decide something like that."

"You're right. After all, you never know who you're going to meet in the snack aisle."

With that, she stood. Cathi set her drink back on the end table, met him where he was, and brought her chest against his. When she saw he wasn't going to seize the moment she'd given, she took the next step. Cathi leaned in and gave him a gentle, testing kiss on the lips. When his eyes opened, he looked her over.

"What brought that on?"

"Nothing particular. Just wanted to do it."

"I'm glad you did."

"Me too."

"By the way," he grinned, "you taste wonderful."

Cathi smiled. "Flatterer." She went to the kitchen and came back with a large bowl for the chips. She poured the whole bag into it, then shoved the bowl into Nate's chest. She liked that chest, but she had to slow their progress just a little. She leaned in and kissed him quick and gentle.

"It's not that I don't trust you. I don't trust myself for a moment. I'm a little hungry, you know?"

"I understand." He turned his whole body away, pointing back toward the open area of the living room. "What's on the radio tonight?"

"Are you kidding?" She moved for the knob and turned the set on. "It's Sunday night!"

In the next moment both their mouths opened, and they said, "Jack Benny!"

To her surprise and delight, rather than retire to an easy chair or even a couch where they could sit together, Nate took the bowl and settled onto the floor in front of the radio. Seeing this, Cathi reached onto the back of the couch for a throw blanket. She kneeled on the floor, and while the tubes on the four-year-old Zenith warmed up and the static began to crackle, she draped the blanket over her shoulders and settled onto the floor beside him.

"Move that," she said of the bowl. Nate put the bowl aside, and she laid her head onto his lap.

As the familiar voice of Don Wilson introduced the Jello Program and the orchestra's first number, she gently shut her eyes as he softly began to stroke her hair.

"I hope he goes into the vault tonight," he said.

She purred, "Why?"

"I don't know," he said quietly. "I guess I like hearing those footsteps descending into the middle of the earth. The doors opening …"

A smile crossed her lips.

"Running into his security guard that's been down there since the Civil War. Hearing all the bells and whistles going off. It's like going somewhere most people aren't allowed. Or, at least, no one gets to see."

"Hey Dingle," she said.

"Yeah?"

"Come down here and curl up with me."

Nate set his tumbler of bourbon aside, slipped off his shoes and slid onto the floor beside her. She threw the blanket over him. There was enough to go around.

Once their bodies were snug, she said, "Now, I'm going to do the second embarrassing thing in the short history of our new relationship."

In a moment, Nate felt a tug at his belt. For the shortest moment, as she began to run her hands along the bare skin of his abdomen, through the coarse hair of his chest, he thought, if this goes on more than a little while I'm going to miss Gildersleeve. Then, feeling a woman's hands run on him in a way he hadn't felt in a long time, the way he had to admit he sorely missed, he decided to relax, let the radio become background noise, and let the rest of the night just happen.

Toothbrush

The moon was the only light in the room when Nate got up to pee.

"Where are you going? You better not be trying to slip out while I'm still awake."

"Gotta do the boy thing."

Cathi crunched her brow a little and shifted her eyes. "What's the boy thing?" she called out toward the room he'd ducked into.

The answer came a few moments later with the sound of a free-flowing stream hitting the bowl. Nate let out a sigh of relief even she could hear. He had visited the pharmacy after all. Maybe it was his crafty way of planting a seed, but either way, it had worked out well for both of them.

He turned the water on to wash his hands, and as he grabbed up the bar of soap—Lux, sponsors of the Lux Radio Hour—and began to wash his hands, something caught his eye. Her toothbrush, or rather, what was left of it.

The lone, red-handled instrument standing alone in the little porcelain cup looked, literally, like something you'd find in the road. The bristles were splayed in every direction except up, flattened by use. A light film of toothpaste had dried in the crevices of the plain, plastic grip on the handle. He wasn't turned off by it;

rather, Nate thought it was one of the most out-of-place things he'd seen in her house.

"Is this the toothbrush you use every day?" he called from the doorway.

Cathi, sitting up in bed, thought a moment. "The red one? Well, I do live alone so, yeah. It's mine. Why?"

Nate carried the worn item into the bedroom.

"What are you doing," she said. "Put that back you goofball. You don't have some weird thing with dental hygiene, do you?"

"No," he said and tapped her lightly on the nose with the worn item. "But I do like your mouth. It works wonderfully."

"Thank you," she smiled. She snatched the brush away and set it on the nightstand.

"But really Cathi, I think it's time for a new toothbrush."

"Can't find one."

"What do you mean you can't find one?"

"Okay, you're going to think this is dumb. But I literally can't find a new *red* toothbrush. I've looked in four cities. All I want," she pointed at the one sitting beside her, "is a basic, basic *red* toothbrush, like that one. Not yellow or brown or with the Pepsodent logo on it. I just want a simple *red* toothbrush. Is that asking too much?"

"Red."

"Yes. Red. Call me insane, but my toothbrushes have always been basic red models. I want a new one, yes. And I've looked far and wide. And guess what?

There seems to be some kind of basic red toothbrush shortage. Everything's all," she tried to think of the word, "complicated."

"Complicated," he repeated.

"Yeah, you know. Some things shouldn't be complicated. And one of them, believe it or not, is your toothbrush."

Nate wasn't deterred. "Why always red?"

"What?"

"Why?"

"Why what?"

"Why always red?"

"Oh! Right. Well, I saw this movie once, the hero gets lost, literally in a field somewhere. And he's got nothing. His belongings are stuffed away, hidden somewhere while he's on the run, right? The only thing he grabbed out of his bag was his toothbrush. A red toothbrush. And he carries it around with him throughout the movie like a security blanket."

"Well," Nate said, "I think your security blanket's a little worn out. So tomorrow, if you're not tired of me, we'll go out and buy you a new toothbrush."

"Okay. But just so you know, I've tried. By the way," she added, "if you ever need a purple or yellow or green toothbrush, there's a pile of unused ones under the sink."

Nate watched her studying the worn out brush and smiled to himself. "You've got a stash of unused, perfectly good toothbrushes in the bathroom and yet you brush your pearly whites with that?"

She demonstrated with a few quick passes at her bicuspids. "You didn't seem to mind when we were making out."

"But now that I know …"

She gasped and smiled at the same time. "Like you don't have any horrible habits I'm going to find out about later."

"Oh, I'm sure there's something that'll be a deal breaker."

"Oh, I'm sure there will be." She gave him a light kiss. "But, who knows? Maybe we'll be the kind of people that work through it."

New Day

The morning came, and with it, Cathi was the first to stir. She tried to wake Nate with her stare, and when that didn't work, she kissed his ear. When that didn't work, she reached under the sheets.

That worked.

It wasn't until the afternoon that they showered and left their love nest. It was a bright Sunday full of possibilities. They waited on the bus that took them to LeGrand's Drug Store, a Rexall pharmacy—sponsors of the Phil Harris & Alice Faye Show—with the big orange and blue letters on the building. Mr. LeGrand was in the middle of the store, straightening a display of comic books.

"Well hello," he said to the newly minted couple.

"Hi, Mr. LeGrand," Nate opened. "This is Cathi."

"We know each other," Cathi smiled.

"Oh sure," the druggist said, "I sell her all her toothpicks. By the way, how are you set for them?"

"Jim Dandy for now," Cathi replied.

"Toothpicks?" Nate said to her.

"I'll explain later."

"And you Mr. Dingle, I'm expecting a fresh shipment from you this week."

"Of course," Nate nodded, "and it'll be on time as always. What's with the mess on the news rack," he pointed.

"Oh, just a neighborhood boy who lives around here. He comes in after school and browses without ever buying. His uncle is a good customer, so I overlook it. Let him read. So long as he can read, you know? So," he refocused on the duo, "what can I do for you today?"

"Toothbrush," Cathi said.

"Red toothbrushes, specifically," said Nate.

LeGrand pointed. "Right over there. You might find a red one. Just got a new shipment two days ago."

Cathi reached the display first. There, right in the front row, standing proud and tall and firm in its little cardboard sleeve was a brand new, red toothbrush.

"It's destiny," Nate said.

"Some days are like this," she nodded.

"Put it on the account?" LeGrand asked. He was behind the register now.

"No, not today. In fact, let's settle accounts." She reached into her handbag and extracted a wallet. "How much is my balance."

LeGrand reached under the counter and pulled out a large ledger, almost half the width of his chest. He flipped open to a page and slid the point of a pencil down to her name.

"Nine dollars and nine cents," he announced. "With the new toothbrush, let's just call it an even ten dollars."

Cathi pulled out a ten dollar bill, slid it across the counter, picked up the toothbrush and dropped it into her purse. "Thank you, Mr. LeGrand."

"And thank you. If you like, the new Radio Mirror came in," he pointed at the rack.

Cathi waved a hand. "Maybe tomorrow. We've gotta get a move on right now."

"And I'll be seeing you later in the week too," Nate waved at the druggist. "Take care."

"Nice seeing you both."

Nate and Cathi stepped onto the sidewalk. Pop's was only a few blocks away.

"What did you mean back there when you said you'd see him later in the week?" Cathi asked.

"Well, I will."

"He said he was expecting a new shipment from you. I suppose this is as good a time as any to ask what you do."

Nate smiled and reached in his coat pocket for his card. Cathi held it up to study, and as she did, she tried to hide her surprise.

The name was correct; Nathan Dingle, Proprietor. The color, the lettering, and name of the company were the same as the one she'd seen the day before—Little Birdie's Bread Company.

Of course, she thought to herself. *A Gildersleeve fan would certainly borrow the name from his favorite show and make a go of it.* She waved the little card around, then stuck it in her purse.

"Now I've got you filed away, Mr. Nathan Dingle."

"And you Miss Cathi … what is your last name?"

Just then, they arrived at their destination. Cathi waved an arm up at the sign of the store's frontage.

"There it is," she said. "The inheritance."

"Inheritance?"

Cathi explained the inheritance, the investment, her interest in Pop's place. She pushed open the front door. Nate followed.

"Impressive. You run your own malt shop."

"I do," Cathi said firmly. They took a table, and seeing his boss with company, Pop came right to their table.

"Hello Miss, how may I serve you?"

"It's okay Pop, you don't have to put on an act. Nathan, this is Pop."

The two men shook hands. "Nathan Dingle," Nate said.

"Hah! Dingle!" Pop said. "Like the forgetful postman."

Nate looked at Cathi. "I need to listen to this show, I think."

"Nathan probably needs a sandwich, don't you, Nathan."

"Oh yes. Do you have turkey?"

"Do I! With cheese and a little mustard."

"That'll be great."

"And I'll have the usual Pop. Nathan and I have a little business to talk over."

Pop took the cue and disappeared into the kitchen.

Nate leaned forward, elbows on the table. "Business?"

Cathi smiled. "I hope you'll find your sandwich up to par," she said.

"I'm sure it'll be fine."

"Even if," she took his card out of her purse, "it is served on inferior bread."

"If it isn't our Little Birdie's bread, then I suppose it's going to be inferior," he joked.

She stared him down.

"What?" he said.

She kept staring. She was sizing up that smile of his, looking to see if it was intentional, to see if she was being bamboozled.

"What's bothering you?" he asked.

She spun the business card between her fingers. "The only thing I know that's inferior about Little Birdie's Bread Company is the quality of some of their employees."

Nate leaned back a little. He wasn't sure where she was going. This aggression. Well, sure, after all she'd done to make moves on him last night, no one could say she wasn't a slightly more than average woman.

"Where is this coming from?" he said. "I don't understand. Have we met in the past and my memory is slipping?"

Cathi looked out the window. The street, the cars, the people moved on as usual.

"You have a distributor named Paul Leonard."

Nate's eyes searched the table, the way a man tends to do when searching the names and contacts in his head.

"Oh, Leonard!" he suddenly remembered. "Yes. He's the new guy. We, uh …"

When he stuttered, she leaned forward a little.

Strange as it was, in those few moments while Nate searched for words, Cathi was thinking only of the toothbrush in her purse. That new, wonderful brush she'd wanted so long and couldn't find. Then this man shows up, and fate drops a new one right into the first drug store he takes her to. It was a symbol of how right things can go when, as he'd said about his grandmother the night before, both a man and woman are rowing in the same direction.

"You what," she helped him along.

"This is confidential, okay. Paul was released from state prison not too long ago. One of his cousins, he's a good guy that wouldn't harm anybody … the cousin I mean, he asked me if we'd help Paul out. Get him back on his feet. I called his parole officer, I then called the warden and asked about the risk I was taking. They both applauded us for giving him a chance. I guess ex-cons, I don't know many, so I don't know all this for sure, but I guess it isn't easy for them to get a job once the state sets them free."

She set the card on the table. "Yeah. Well, you'd think that when someone puts their name on the line for you and goes through all that trouble, you think they'd treat that opportunity with a bit more respect."

Nate shook his head again. "I don't get this. How do you know Paul?"

"I don't. He came in here last night and introduced himself. He didn't make a real good impression."

"Oh?"

"You might say I appreciate a man with strong arms, but I don't appreciate someone trying to strongarm *me*." She looked him in the eye. "Do you understand what I'm telling you?"

Nate sat upright. He nodded lightly.

"I'm sorry we had to talk to each other like this," she said.

Nate kept nodding. "So am I."

Pop brought their food, along with a couple of Cokes.

Nate thanked Pop, then looked down at the seat beside him. He picked up the hat that had been lying on the cushion. He ran his fingers along the new felt of its brim.

"I'll understand whatever you decide. But I'm going to tell you right now, I have only one thing on my mind at the moment, Cathi."

She had one elbow on the table. She didn't know what she wanted to hear at that precise moment, but somewhere deep inside her, she hoped he knew what it was.

"While you were telling me this, while I was hearing you say it ... I was thinking of only one thing. All day long, I've felt like I was the most important man in the world. At least, in the little world we've had. And I'm not going to leave it until you tell me to. I'll fight anyone for my right to be here. Because, Cathi, the thing that matters most to me in life right now ..."

Nate reached into her bag. He extracted the toothbrush and set it on the table.

"That's fate. You say you've been looking a long time? Well, I've been looking a long time for something too. And I'm not going to let anything, especially some cheap hood get in my way. I know how to push back."

Cathi nodded. "I feel the same way."

"Now," he said calmly. "Here's what my day is going to look like. First, I'm going to eat this turkey sandwich—"

"On inferior bread," she said.

"On inferior bread. Then I'm going to my bakery, and I'm going to find a foreman that's worked for me for ten years. He's the kind of man I can trust and the kind of man who follows orders. I'm going to assign Leonard to him. And eventually, he's going to see Leonard screw up somewhere. After I talk to my foreman today, I'm going to walk up to my office. And I'm going to open my desk drawer, and I'm going to fill out a pink slip with Leonard's name on it. And I'm going to leave the date blank. It's going to be a matter of time before I'm filling it in."

Cathi nodded.

"Then, later this evening, I'm going to come by your house. And I'm going to bring you two things. First off, I'll have a dozen roses so the house will smell like our love all week long."

Cathi smiled. "What's the other thing?"

Nate took a bite of his sandwich. "A loaf of Little Birdie's bread. You've gotta get rid of this stuff."

Cathi laughed lightly.

"Then around eight o'clock," he continued, "we're going to lie next to the radio. And you're going to bring your favorite blanket. And we're going to listen to The Shadow."

'*Who knows … what evil … lurks in the hearts of men,*' she heard the opening line speed through her head. She nodded.

"That sounds wonderful," she said. And it did. Then, something came past that filter that the nuns had tried to place in her throat.

"Just one thing Nathan. I'm not sure I'm designed to be someone's wife. Maybe not for a while. Or who knows, maybe ever. It just doesn't appeal to me. You appeal to me. But marriage …"

"We don't have to talk about these things."

"Thank you."

"It's one of the things of our generation. So many things belong down the road. Answers don't all have to be right in front of us. We're in no rush. In fact, I think it's fair to say that the less we rush, the happier we're likely to be. Don't you think?"

Cathi looked around the little malt shop. Pop's was a success again. It was something she'd resurrected, reinvented, the way Fanny had done for herself after she'd left the Follies. Cathi knew now that all she wanted, in the end, was to be happy. She looked at this man, looking back at her across the table. He made her happy. She didn't need to marry him to feel that happiness.

She knew she wouldn't mind curling up beside him, hearing his voice, letting it take the place of the white noise her radio had provided all these years as she'd waited for him to come along. *Yes,* she thought, *his voice would certainly do. Maybe for a little while, anyway.*

Expired Sicilian

Joanna Bair

Josephine braced herself as her train pulled into the Bagheria train station. The short ride from Palermo had not been nearly enough time to prepare herself for the wrath of Papa. Thirty-five years old and still no husband after three years in America, after he'd threatened to kill her for going with a policeman, who he'd subsequently killed. She stepped off the platform and breathed in the humid salt air. A man offered to carry her luggage, but she shook her head, "No."

She didn't trust anyone in this town. Not after how she'd left.

Papa's villa stood on the same street as the train station, not much farther down the road. Men huddled in doorways chatting in voices that to a stranger might sound like arguing. She laughed to herself, some things never changed. The balconies with laundry draped out to dry in the sun brought a flash of New York to her mind, but the limestone buildings didn't begin to compare with the brick tenements of New York.

"*Giuseppina, Giuseppina!*" an older lady rushed out to greet her. "*Bellisima*, you've grown, so beautiful, so fat."

The lady grabbed her hand, "No husband? I knew you'd come home. There will never be another Francesco, God rest his soul."

Josephine glanced around her to make sure no one in the family could see her talking to Francesco's *nona*. She had come home to bring peace if possible, not stir up trouble. She ignored the comments and kissed her old boyfriend's grandmother on each cheek. "It's lovely to see you again."

"Be sure to tell me how your father is. No one knows anymore. They say he's suffered greatly since his children left."

"It's his own fault," Giuseppina nodded and waved.

"Don't let him kill you!" Nona called after her.

She shuddered, fear shaking her bones. *Agata had said he was too weak to kill.*

She focused her eyes on the rubble in front of her eyes. She'd expected ruins, but not her entire street demolished from the war. Her gaze fixed on the front gates to her father's villa. The barren yard, void of grass sat at the bottom of rolling hills heading north toward the sea. The orange trees looked sparse, but a few stood scattered standing nowhere near as tall as the villa. Palm trees had grown up against the gate, and she pushed away fronds to enter. She sucked in a deep breath, she'd trusted the man inside this villa with her life, until three years ago. She'd known no one crossed his path, not even his daughter was exempt. *What would he do now?* From what she heard his body was too frail.

"*Giuseppina!*" Agata, their maid, ran out to meet her.

"Jo," she corrected her, used to the American diminutive of Josephine, not sure if she'd answer to *Giuseppina* all the time, it had been so long.

"No, *Giuseppina, bienvenuto,* welcome," she ushered her inside the gates. The enormous white villa in front of her would house hundreds in New York City. Up close she felt small against the home she'd grown up in, she'd forgotten her family's wealth. *How much of it had been earned honestly?* Likely none she suddenly realized.

Agata chattered away in Italian, "Your Papa will be pleased to see you, even if he doesn't act it. He will be angry, after all you and your brother put him through, avoiding the draft, then you leaving to join him when the bombs began. I am so happy you were spared."

"I'm happy you are safe," Josephine told the maid. "But Papa, is he really truly going to be happy to see me? I don't know how he will react. You and I both know we didn't leave because of the war."

"He's weak, and no one else agrees with his decision to kill you. You'd be dead already if they did. He won't hurt you. He doesn't have it in him, or he'd have done the deed three years ago when you ran off with that policeman. His guns are hidden. You can say your goodbyes and leave if you like, but it's such a long journey. I hope you stay. I can't believe you've found it in yourself to forgive him." Agata raised her eyebrows searching Josephine's face. Josephine looked away not wanting Agata to read her thoughts in case they gave her away.

"The Scadutos are strong. Not like your name, you aren't failures at all." Agata said referring to Josephine's family name which meant 'expired' or 'failure at life.' She'd been teased all her life about that name.

"You will expire, like our name." her father had said before they'd escaped for America.

He'd meant to insult them, but Josephine and her brother, Angelo had no respect for their father anymore.

"But you'll expire an old maid," Francesco's *nona* had said when she'd left for America, *but better that than die.*

Agata waved her hand across the street toward the ruins changing the subject to the war. "You know the DiLeos and Castiglianos were not so lucky."

Josephine nodded but didn't say anything more. Agata took her suitcase to carry to her room, she studied Josephine's attire, "Trousers? Is that what women in America wear now, too? Your Papa is in his office."

"*Grazie*," Josephine thanked Agata then ran across the slippery tile floor almost skidding to a stop before her father's office. She'd forgotten how slick tile was after all the hardwood in America.

"Papa," she knocked softly on the door.

"*Giuseppina?*" she heard a low voice and pushed open the door.

"Oh Papa," she glanced at him realizing he sat in a wheelchair, "Agata never wrote it was this bad."

"You are dead to me," Papa stated and turned the chair around.

"I know Papa. I came to say I'm sorry," she said quietly.

"If I weren't stuck in this chair, you'd be gone, you know."

"I know. I never would have returned, but Agata pleaded." Josephine hoped her lie wouldn't throw the maid under a bus. "I'll do anything you ask."

He turned his chair, eyes in a doubtful glare, "Truly? You've come to your senses?"

She nodded. "I never should have disobeyed you in the first place. If I had married Marco like you'd wanted I never would have met Francesco, and he would still be alive. But what's done is done. Papa, it's been years, would you please forgive me?"

"Will you truly marry Marco? He's still available. No one ever married him," Papa said.

"Because he's … not now Papa. Can we not talk about marriage?" she sighed.

"I need someone to carry on my name. I can't just leave this villa to anyone," he leaned back in his chair.

"So you've said," she looked around.

"And I certainly can't leave it to a female," Papa said.

"Of course not," Josephine said. "Angelo—"

"Is dead. So, will you do it?"

"What?"

"Marry Marco," Papa shouted, his frustration building. This was her cue to exit.

"I'll consider it," Josephine turned to leave, wheels rolling in her head. "It's good to see you Papa, and Angelo is not dead. He said he's praying for you."

"He's dead," her father shouted, "and if you're not careful I'll be demanding you're next."

"Papa, no one will agree to my death. You and I both know it. Good night." She said.

Before she closed the door her father turned quiet, "are the streets in America really paved with gold?"

"Of course not, and New York City is just as hot and humid in the summer. But we get snow up to our waists sometimes. Can you imagine?"

He shook his head with a smile, "I can't."

Josephine smiled and closed the door. There's no way she could marry Marco. If she did she'd have to kill him, but then she would be just like her father. She wanted no part in the mafia, and Marco would be the top Don one day. She should have stayed in America. But her inheritance. It couldn't stay in the mafia. It was rightly hers and Angelo's, and she would make sure it stayed that way.

Josephine wove her way through the throngs of people in the ballroom. Mainly relatives, here to glimpse the thought-to-be-dead daughter of Signor

Scaduto. Far from expired, she received attention from many young eyes, yet none as good looking as Francesco. She'd already determined in her mind to never marry. Not after all the drama and certainly not if it meant more lives were at stake.

"*Giuseppina*, you remember Marco," Papa motioned to the man next to him. She nodded. How could she forget the one man who teased her about expiring long before she actually had in anyone's eyes?

"*Bella*," the man nodded.

Since when did he think me beautiful? Clearly her father's influence. If she convinced her father they were in love, perhaps he'd leave her alone, and include her in his will once again. A marriage to Marco could offer her protection and security for all her life if she decided to stay in Sicily. In truth, she'd returned to reconcile and get back what was rightly hers. She sighed. She'd vowed to never marry, but perhaps an exception needed to be made.

"It's been a long time."

"Not nearly long enough," Josephine muttered in English.

"*Scusi?*" the man asked.

"Oh, yes, it's been years. How have you been?" Josephine asked genuinely interested in the man's assets and accomplishments. She needed to know if she could trust him to be dimwitted enough to dupe.

"The oranges on my plantation haven't been producing quite as well, so I turned to machinery during the war. It's been quite lucrative." Marco's chest puffed out his muscles as he spoke, and Josephine held back a snort.

"So, you've become a businessman. Respectable." Josephine smiled, pressing her hand to smooth her turquoise silk gown. Her other hand twirled a strand of pearls nervously, a lot was at stake on this meeting for all of them.

"Barely. Now the war is over there's no need for so much to be produced. I've gone back to oranges, but I'll inherit my father's estate. I have nothing to worry about. Just a wife and family to pass everything on to. But what of you? You disgraced your father you know, by siding with the allies." His eyes narrowed as he spoke.

"I did not side with anyone in the war. I sided with life. I chose to live." Josephine retorted though she needed to stay on this man's good side. If he showed enough potential, he would be her next ally. In that case, she wanted him understanding her motive, to a degree.

"You went against your father did you not? And he's the most dedicated fascist in Bagheria." Marco took her elbow and pulled her to a corner of the room. It would appear to the rest of the room an interest had sparked between the two.

"I don't care much for politics. I chose love. Nearly thirty years old I felt I would have no other prospects, so it never mattered to me what he believed. I'm sure you understand." Josephine put on a remorseful voice and added, "But I see the error of my ways."

"*Alora,* well then, that is good to hear. I was concerned when your papa asked me to pursue you, but I see you're like most women, uninterested in the affairs of men."

Cringing inside, but giving Marco a coquettish wink of agreement she took his hand. "Shall we dance?"

The music had grown into a lively jitterbug reminding her of the clubs in New York. The longer she stayed here, the more she realized how much she'd changed in that city, while aside from the ruins and heartache of war, much had stayed the same at home. She wasn't even sure she could call it home anymore. The same men meandered to and fro about the party. Dark suits, loud voices, debating politics, plotting revenge, seeking allies. The same families feuding, many not invited to her home. Of course, no one from Francesco's family came. All because of a century-old feud. Not that her dating him had helped bring peace. Instead, she'd made things worse. Her own father had killed her only love.

She'd much prefer to be spending the evening with Francesco's *nona.* But she couldn't be seen with her anymore unless she wanted to be dead herself. She'd never forgive her father for his threats to her own life. *Never.* And she didn't trust a word he said. She wouldn't until she had that will with her name on it in her hand.

She longed for America with its Irish, Italians, Germans, and races of all kinds coming together under one roof to support the war effort. Sure some looked down on immigrants, but for the most part, she'd been welcomed. She couldn't fathom such a mix of people coming together in her father's house. Everyone suspicious of one another constantly judged their lifelong neighbors. As long as the mafia stood, there'd be none of that.

She kicked her legs out to the front, side, and rocked her feet back and forth holding Marco's hand. Dancing always released stress, and she found herself having fun with Marco. His feet moved with agility, and he seemed to be enjoying himself. She couldn't take down the mafia single-handedly, so she may as well join them. She'd be set for life and able to leave for New York with the money when she had her chance. She'd get Marco to marry her so she could inherit her villa. She saw now it was her only option. She'd deal with everything else later. She knew his type. He was after her inheritance as well. There was no question about that, but she'd make sure he never saw a penny.

"What did you do in America?" Marco asked her a few weeks later as they strolled along the coastal shore of nearby Aspra Mare.

"I sang," she answered dipping her toes in the water.

"You made money singing?" She couldn't tell if he looked impressed or amused.

"I did. I sang on an Italian radio station and in clubs." She shrugged.

"In Italian?" He asked.

"Of course, the only songs I knew when I arrived were in Italian," she answered. "Though I learned others. Everyone wanted entertainment to forget about the war."

He nodded. "You never did that here. I'm not sure I knew you could sing. Dance yes, but sing, no."

He took her into his arms as if to dance. She let him guide her along the dark sand, an almost reddish color from the clay.

"You never got drafted, how come?" She asked Marco, weaving her fingers with his.

"I had seizures as a child, do you remember? I thought I'd outgrown them, but when the bombing started, they returned. The doctors thought stress had made me worse again. I found ways to serve here. I would have gone to war, I was not a coward like your brother." Marco said. If he was trying to upset her, it was working, but she couldn't let him know.

"Would you ever go to America?" She ignored the comment about her brother being a coward and moved to more important questions. Instead of stepping away from him she pulled him close to her. They'd spent most evenings together since the ball, but he'd yet to kiss her. Tonight she would make sure he did. Bagheria was growing on her again, but she was anxious to return to New York and start her life over again.

"No, everything I want is right here. Why? Are you going back?" He studied her carefully.

"No, everything left is here for me too." She lied expertly. All those months of singing on stage had improved her acting ability. Josephine attempted to see if Marco's expression changed when she mentioned her father's sickness. It didn't, but he pulled her even closer, so she could feel his heart racing against her chest. "Life as a singer is not as glamorous as it sounds. Besides, with Papa failing, I know I need to be here, regardless of whether or not he recovers."

"I am glad you're staying," he grinned, his breath warm on her face, she closed her eyes and felt his lips touch hers as if to seal the agreement. They would inherit the villa. She could tell he wanted it as badly as she did.

Papa's health declined rapidly, the cancer spreading throughout his body, confining him to bed. His immune system weakened, and he caught a cold which turned to pneumonia with coughing fits that scared even the toughest men who came to visit him. They all knew his time was coming, but the town also knew a wedding was coming.

"We should marry soon, so your father can be there," Marco said, and Josephine agreed.

Agata gloried in planning the wedding, "Finally!"

Lawyers came to the villa putting everything in order. The will now had their names on it and children of theirs, though there wouldn't be any, would inherit the villa. Affairs in order, the wedding was scheduled for autumn, but Papa never made it past summer. Instead, arrangements were made for a funeral, the villa sold, and money put safely in Marco's villa where the two would live. The wedding was not postponed.

Violins played as Josephine's strides took her down the path to Papa's villa—now hers. Oranges lined the walkway as she strained to see through the white veil covering her face. An ache filled her heart as she walked solo down the aisle. She'd hated Papa, but she felt his absence. Agata sat in the front row ready to uncover her veil when she reached her. Today she'd become Signora Marco Abela.

The priest's words blurred in her head, but she repeated the vows. "Til death do us part." Time stood still as the words sunk in.

"I now pronounce you man and wife."

Marco kissed her passionately, one thing she couldn't complain about, even if she was emotionally detached, she'd miss that aspect of him. They raced down the aisle, and the celebration continued with eight courses of food. Antipasto, insalata, pasta, fish, meat, desserts, and the list went on. Josephine only picked at each course, yet somehow wound up full. Appetites gone, and the men drunk on wine from nearby vineyards, the party dwindled. The band left, and guests said their farewells.

"Shall we go home?" Marco held out a hand, his look ravenous toward her. She hadn't decided if she'd let him have a wedding night or not. Her plan from the beginning had been to take the money and run, but Papa's stipulation on the will stated if she were to divorce the money would go to Marco. She couldn't have that.

Her brother and her needed the money in America. They'd run the hottest club in New York City. They'd be the life of the party, of the city, and they'd have no need to work again. Or they'd buy a house upstate, start their own orchards, maybe apples. There were options again.

She wasn't brave enough or stupid enough to shoot her husband. He'd die from food poisoning at the wedding. No one would trace it back to her. She'd already been putting bits of arsenic in his drinks for days. She followed Marco to his villa, a short walk down the street from hers.

"You're quiet tonight," he said kissing her hand.

"I'm exhausted," she answered. Stepping into his empty villa, he led her upstairs to the bedroom. She'd had Agata bring the bottle of wine with arsenic for her, along with a few others for cover.

"The night has only begun," Marco smiled mischievously, and Josephine wondered what went on in his mind.

"So it has," she said, "turn around so I can change."

"I'll be back," he took his cue, and she poured two glasses of wine from two very different bottles. Marco returned in a navy silk robe with gold trim. She strolled over to him, her dressing gown fluttering open. She held a glass out to him, "More wine?"

He took it.

"To us," she clinked her glass to his and took a sip. He drank, and she waited. He needed to drink more.

"I feel funny," he looked at her.

"You're tired as well. Here. The wine will help." She offered more, and he sipped slowly staring her down. She smiled, and he set aside the glass lowering her to the bed beginning to kiss and caress her passionately. She responded until she felt something hard against her leg and froze. In a flash, Marco's body was on top of her, a pistol in his hand, placed at her head.

"Tonight, *ma donna*, you are going to drown in the sea when you fall off my yacht. Your body will disappear forever." He kissed her. "But first, you are my wife. You protest or scream, and I shoot."

She didn't dare move or say a thing. She waited for the arsenic to take effect and slowly he began groaning. "My stomach."

"Anxiety my dear. You won't really shoot me, you couldn't possibly. Everyone will know I didn't drown."

"No one will care. Your father should have done away with you when you first went against the family. A policeman? What were you thinking? You were expired, like your name, from the moment you chose that man. He would have been the death of your father. You never had concern for your family." He grabbed the glass of wine with his other hand and sipped, "I'm so thirsty."

He gagged and ran to the bathroom taking the pistol with him. She followed and rubbed his back as he threw up into the toilet.

"Stupid girl, thinking you could outwit the mafia and get my money." He choked. "Don't just stand here, go get help. I'm sick."

"You must have eaten too much," Josephine suggested. He didn't respond but was sick again. Josephine didn't leave the room.

"Go! Get a doctor!" He yelled at her.

"I don't want to leave you." She said. He held his pistol up to her again but fell over in pain. She waited for him to ride out the cramps, but this time they didn't end. Instead, his body went limp. Quickly she removed the pistol from his hand, checked his pulse and threw it in her bag. She ran from the room.

"Agata, Agata, anyone? Marco is sick!" The servants came running. In the chaos, she slipped off into the office. Picking up the suitcase of money from the safe she grabbed her other bag of clothing and left in the night. Putting her hat low over her eyes she walked briskly to the sea.

Marco's yacht gleamed in the moonlight. She'd risk the short trip to Malta and eventually fly to America from there. Francesco's *nona* waited on the shore for her.

They'd had their revenge. She handed the old lady a stack of bills.

"*Grazie mille*, now be safe," the old lady kissed each cheek. "My niece in Malta will hide you in their bomb shelter if needed. Don't write to me though. It's too dangerous. Now go, Francesco's brother is on the yacht waiting. He'll get you there safely. You may be expired to Sicilia, but not to the rest of the world."

The Fly Girl

E. W. Farnsworth

This story is true, with names changed to protect identities.

Midge Ryder wore her attitude into every room. Today in the ballroom of the Waldorf Astoria Hotel, converted into a makeshift lecture hall, she was the main speaker and guest of the Rockefellers. Her topic was "Flying the World Over—and Female!" She had the creds. The initial applause as she approached the lectern was resounding. Emelia was standing toward the rear, beaming from ear to ear. They had flown together frequently in those days, and they were known for other exploits less public but sensitive and important from the national point of view.

For example, Ryder and Earhart, in that order, infiltrated Nazi Germany to gauge the mettle of the rising star named Adolf Hitler. They termed him a dangerous demagogue, buoyed on the sentiments of a defeated people longing to be great again. Because of their being single women of the leisure class, they could rub elbows with the upper crust in the Great Depression without having to make excuses for never having been married.

"Being single has its advantages," Midge said as she looked around the room full of young women hoping to hear advice from a successful woman in difficult times. In the front row of the audience, sat twelve dour male newspaper reporters, smoking cigarettes and pipes as if laying down a smoke screen between the speaker and her audience. They applauded between episodes of derision and disbelief. For them and their readers, Midge was a curiosity. The mystery, in their sexist opinionated minds, was not that Midge Ryder could do everything a man could do, better but that she could do so many things at all.

Throughout her set speech, Miss Ryder wondered why she had been asked to address this group of fans. She had the distinct impression she was being put under a microscope by someone, but she could not guess the purpose. She gave up trying to guess about the matter, and her thoughts became fixed on the afterparty in the Tea Room, where all should become clear.

She ended her speech with a rousing call to young women everywhere, "To dare to do!" Her peroration was a feminist cry in the wilderness to all young women who felt a call beyond traditional subservience within the circle of marriage and the family. When she ended and fell silent, the women in the audience rose in a standing ovation, cheering and clapping with abandon. Midge nodded and looked right for the fastest way off the dais. Her intention was to whisk through the crowd to her place in the receiving line, shake hands perfunctorily and escape to the street.

In the receiving line, she was flanked by two scions of the Rockefellers, both eligible males. She paid them no attention but politely passed the well-wishers down the line firmly. She hated small talk, but she knew the drill.

Her patron shook her hand and cut her out of the line. "Wouldn't you like a gin and tonic for this heat?"

She felt relieved to be escorted early to the Tea Room by a married gentleman of unquestioned integrity. As he arranged for their drinks, he looked around to be sure no one was in hearing.

"A guest is waiting for you upstairs in Room 445. When we've had our drinks, I'll take you to him."

"With all the press, I hope this can be managed discreetly." Her meaning did not escape him. Miss Ryder was careful about her reputation, and she was also careful of the reputations of all those she met.

"Don't worry. I'll be careful how I manage this. So far, no one knows the old man is here. We had a special device to deliver your speech to his room, so he knows your message. It is his message to you that you need to hear. I must warn you that two men will be present in the room … and that should be some comfort to you."

"This is all so mysterious. Later this afternoon, I'm going flying. Will the interview take long?"

Rockefeller's eyebrow raised a fraction. "That all depends on how things are going among you." T

he server brought two drinks, and the doors opened so the other guests could enter and mill about. They kept a respectful distance from the great man and his apparent protégé.

Rockefeller nodded to a few people he knew while Miss Ryder matched him sip for sip, so both finished their drinks at the same moment. He nodded that it was time. He led, and she followed him out the door to the hotel lobby.

Two large, handsome men closed on the pair to keep others away as they navigated toward the elevator which took them to the fourth floor. Rockefeller knocked three times on the door of Room 445, which opened on a handsome young newspaperman whom Midge knew and a man in a wheelchair, whom everyone in the world knew—F. D. Roosevelt.

Rockefeller performed the introductions, and then he withdrew, leaving the three alone.

"Miss Ryder, I won't waste your time with pleasantries. I have a task for you, and if you should choose to undertake it, I will discuss it with you only as long as it takes for you to grasp the gist of it. After that, it will be up to you and Mr. Byrd to execute it and report back to me. You are to keep my name entirely out of your mind as you perform your job, and I shall avoid giving the press any inkling of your mission for me. Is that clear?"

"Yes, Mr. President, it is."

"Would you two like a drink with alcohol before we begin?"

"No, thank you," the two young people said simultaneously.

"Well, then, be seated. I'll begin. If you have any questions, please wait until I've finished."

Ryder and Byrd sat at the small table opposite Roosevelt and leaned forward to hear what he had to say.

"I suppose you are aware that the Jews are particularly worried about what's happening in Germany. I also suppose you know about British plans to provide a Jewish homeland for them in Palestine. What I need you to investigate is another possible venue for the Jewish homeland—in Ethiopia. That's your mission in a nutshell. I cannot overemphasize its sensitivity. I must ask right now whether you are willing to accept the mission."

Both young people nodded.

"Well, then," the president said, "let's all have a cigarette to discuss it. I won't bore you with signing papers that you will keep secret all details of this mission—to the grave."

The three lit up their cigarettes, Roosevelt using his cigarette holder to keep the smoke out of his eyes.

"I don't think it will take you long to become instant experts on the historical situation, so I'll assume you'll do your homework and get right to the crux. Adolf Hitler has a plan to exterminate the Jews throughout Europe. Important Jews are aware of this, and mass migration is their answer—for their survival. The problem with that is, there are limits to the numbers of Jews any country can permit. I include the United States. I assure you, my administration will do all it can, but we have our own anti-Semite faction, which is sympathetic to the Nazi program. So, the future Jewish homeland must have three features. It must have land for settlement. It must have some connection to the Jewish people. It must have a regime that is willing—or could be induced—to open its doors to Jewish immigrants."

"Mr. President, why did you choose us, of all people, to execute this secret mission? Surely, it is more appropriate for the Department of State?" As Byrd asked this question, Ryder became aware the newshound had no more prior knowledge of the mission than she had.

"My advisers pointed me in your direction as two people of utmost discretion, who have already performed secret missions for those at the highest level of this government. You also have backgrounds that make you most suitable. A newspaper man and a flyer would be a natural pair to collaborate on a feature article. You, Byrd, are fluent in many languages, including Arabic. You, Miss Ryder, are familiar with flight protocols in North Africa and the Middle East. Besides, Mr. Rockefeller has checked your backgrounds thoroughly. Neither of you has any discernible vices. And you aren't trammeled by family."

Ryder knit her brow. "You mentioned a final report. What do you envision that would contain? And how will we deliver it seeing that we can't connect ourselves with you after this meeting?"

"Excellent questions. The report need only be typed as points on a single sheet of paper. Make no copies. Deliver the original in an envelope by hand to the man whose name appears on this card." Roosevelt handed each the same business card. "I'm entrusting you each with this information. One can never be sure how secure a mission like this is, but I want the best chance of getting a report from one of you in case the other does not return."

Byrd asked, "When do you want the report to be handed to your representative?"

Roosevelt blew his smoke toward the ceiling. "I was thinking thirty days starting tomorrow. Would that interval be time enough for you to complete your mission?"

Both Byrd and Ryder nodded.

"Oh, yes, I took the liberty of having passports issued as if you are man and wife." The president pushed a passport toward each. The appropriate visas had been stamped on them. "It seemed to us that a husband and wife team would be credible. If you should travel as single persons, questions might arise about your relationship. We could not risk your being arrested for being deviants."

Ryder looked at Byrd, and he shrugged.

"As long as Mr. Byrd doesn't get any odd ideas from this arrangement, I can live with it."

Roosevelt grinned. He stubbed his cigarette out. The others did likewise with theirs. Byrd and Ryder stood.

"Thank you for agreeing to undertake this vital mission. Good luck to both of you. Just knock on the door, and Mr. Rockefeller will escort you to the lobby. Remember, we never met. And from the moment you leave this hotel, you two are married, unofficially of course."

Ryder excused herself to change in the ladies' room just off the hotel lobby. Byrd changed in the gents'. Ten minutes later Byrd and Ryder, both in comfortable outdoor clothing, shared a taxi to the airport.

"I think we should be on first name basis now that we're married," Byrd said. "My name is Harold."

"I'll call you Harry. Why don't you call me Midge?"

"While you're flying around the countryside this afternoon, I intend to go to the New York Public Library to do research. I'll keep your dress clothes and return them to you later if you like."

"That's fine with me. Why not meet at my apartment for dinner at eight o'clock this evening? Oh, dear, isn't that awfully forward of me?" She handed him her personal card.

"Not at all, Mrs. Byrd." He read her card and nodded.

She punched him playfully on the bicep. "That slug will be the extent of our physical relationship, Mr. Byrd."

"I don't suppose you can ever tell me about your former exploits any more than I can tell you about mine."

"If by that you mean my work for the U.S. government, certainly not. As a matter of fact, I should say, 'What exploits?'"

Harry laughed. Midge laughed too. She leapt out of the taxi when it stopped by her plane. He watched as she expertly started her vehicle and signaled him to pull her chocks. She had no sooner lifted off than he was back in the cab headed for the library.

As she flew over the New York countryside, she shook her head in disbelief. To herself, she said, "Today I met the president, who gave me a secret mission to find a homeland for the Jews. I also met a young reporter, a gentleman, who is now on paper my husband. Of course, that legend about my being his wife is pure bunkum. Still, I'm glad he's handsome and looks refined—and he's a linguist as well as an adventurer. Over dinner, I'll find out more about him though I'll not get the chance to talk again with the president. Mr. Rockefeller is, of course, at the bottom of all this. If he had not approved and recommended us, we'd know nothing of this mission. Time will tell whether we all chose well. As for dangers, they could not be much wilder than the risks I take every time I lift off in an airplane."

That evening right on time, Harry knocked on her door. He carried her dress on a hanger and in his other hand carried his notebook. Over a dinner of roast chicken and rice with white wine, Harry told Midge what he had learned.

"It seems, a small Jewish community exists in Ethiopia. Their traditions are ancient, and they have a separate tradition of scriptural interpretation from the Jews who remained in the Middle East."

She said, "So, we need only find the community and talk with the rabbi. We'll poke around for a week or so and return with our report. It all sounds too easy."

"There is a catch," Harry said while looking into his wine.

"Okay, what's the catch?"

"The catch is the Nazis are looking for ancient Jewish artifacts, and they are active in Ethiopia on the scent of some kind of terrific find—no less than the Ark of the Covenant, which the faithful carry in a procession through Aum every year."

"Okay, so we'll steer clear of the Nazi artifact hunters."

"I'm afraid the Nazis may hold sway over the current government of Ethiopia. That could be a show stopper."

"Our mission is to investigate and report our findings, positive or negative."

He squinted, still intent on his wine. "I was really hoping we'd find the alternative the president was hoping for."

Harry and Midge spent the remainder of their evening planning their expedition. Midge explained her flight plan. "Harry, you can fly with me or book a separate passage, so we can meet in front of St. Mary's Church in Aum in ten days. It would be safer for our mission for us to go separately."

He brooded for a while on what she said and nodded. "Okay. I'll book separately and see you in Aum. Whoever gets there first will find lodgings for both of us and establish our legend." When he departed, Harry thanked her for dinner and shook her hand.

Ten days later, Midge Ryder arrived in Aum after an air odyssey that might have been its own travel story. Harry Byrd was already in the village, having taken two rooms in the home of one of the villagers. The old woman who let the rooms was a font of information about the Jews who lived in the area. She had been prepared for the arrival of Byrd's wife, and she helped them celebrate their reunion with a special meal of roast goat meat.

"What have you learned while I was flying?" Midge asked.

"The Nazis have been here and gone, having found nothing of interest."

"I thought the Ark of the Covenant was here. That is just the kind of artifact Hitler would love to harvest."

Harry smiled. "Real artifacts don't have the appearance of imaginative ones. When you see the Ark in the villagers' procession tomorrow night, you'll know what I mean."

"So, we've been invited to the procession?"

"Yes. We'll be participants. We won't have speaking parts, but we've been invited to join in the chanting by torchlight."

"What's the connection between the Christian church and the Jewish artifact?"

Harry explained, "Ethiopian Judaism is not particular about the ownership of the artifact. In fact, it seems the Ark's survival has as much to do with Christianity as with Judaism. I'm not sure the Nazis have entirely given up on seizing the Ark." He brought out a revolver and set it on the table. "Did you come armed?"

Midge reached under her pull-over and revealed her own revolver. "Will this do?"

"It will do only if you can shoot straight. My grandmother was named Annie Oakley, so I learned to shoot before I could read."

Midge smiled. "I'm impressed. Annie Oakley was a personal heroine of mine. I'm not a markswoman, but I can hit a man or woman in the chest or head at ten paces."

While they were examining the interior of St. Mary's Church, Midge saw one of the Nazi spies. Harry advised her to ignore the man, but the man was intrusive.

"What is your interest here?" the German asked.

Harry said in German, "We are writing an article on Aum for a major American magazine."

"Are you going to write about the Ark of the Covenant?"

"Probably not, but we shall be writing about the religious procession that is supposed to happen tonight."

Midge, who knew German well, chimed in, "What are you looking for here?"

The Nazi would not meet her gaze. He said, "I'm looking for anything my leader might find interesting for the Third Reich."

Byrd said, "You won't find anything of interest here. A few crude artifacts, perhaps, but nothing worthy of notice."

The Nazi sniffed. "That is for me to decide. Meanwhile, stay out of my way." He pushed past the Byrds to investigate every cranny of the church. As he turned to force his way out of the church, he muttered, "Jewish rituals have no interest for my leader."

Byrd did not know where the man was heading, but he hoped the German would find his way out of Aum before the procession.

Ryder said, "I'll follow him. Meanwhile, you keep a lookout for other Nazis. I doubt he is alone if he wants to make trouble."

Midge followed the Nazi to the edge of the village where a rope bridge extended over a deep chasm. The

German was halfway across the bridge when he turned with his pistol drawn. Midge raised her hands slowly.

"Why are you threatening me? I've done nothing to you?"

"You Americans have not fooled me. I know why you are here."

"And why is that?" Midge asked.

"You are here to find a homeland for Jews. That is my intelligence. My leader warned us that you would be coming."

"That's nonsense. We're writing a magazine article, as we told you earlier."

"You won't return to deliver your article. I'm going to see to that." He raised his gun, but he was not ready for Midge to drop to her knees and take out her revolver. She fired twice, and the Nazi fell into the chasm.

Harry ran up to see whether Midge was all right.

"I'm okay, but the German seems to have lost his footing when I fired. I don't think I hit him with either shot."

Harry looked into the chasm. The German was sprawled motionless on the rocks at the bottom. When the old woman came to see what had happened, she told Harry, "That evil man has met with his fate. If his companions come looking for him, I'll know what to show them."

That night the procession was held as planned. The Byrds carried torches and marched with the villagers through the pathway in front of the church. Midge thought it odd to hear Ethiopian being spoken while the Ark of the Covenant was borne by the crowd. In the torchlight, Midge saw the robes of the faithful flow in the wind. After the procession, the old woman led the Byrds back to their rooms where she fed them a great feast of celebration.

"We are glad you came," she said. "The Germans came to pillage. They came for the Ark of the Covenant. You stopped them. For that, we will be forever grateful."

The next day two Germans came looking for their companion. The priest who officiated at St. Mary's took them to the edge of the chasm. He explained how the man "just fell from the rope bridge." The two Germans shook their heads.

One of the Germans said, "We'll have to report this incident."

The old woman said, "You do that. State the truth—that the man was clumsy. He tried to turn on the rope bridge, lost his footing and fell. Once that happens, there is nothing to break the fall until you reach the bottom."

The Nazis debated how they were going to retrieve the body from the chasm. They fashioned a long rope, which one of them held in the middle of the rope bridge while the other rappelled down. During the attempt, the one on the bridge lost his footing, and both he and his partner fell to the bottom of the chasm. Now three men lay dead. The priest decided to report the deaths as occurring in an unfortunate climbing accident in a treacherous place. He requested assistance from Germany to retrieve the bodies so they might be returned to their fatherland.

The Ethiopian government official who came to investigate told Harry, "Such accidents do happen from time to time. Our government will inform the Germans and request their aid. Such delicate matters take time. The official did not wink at Harry, but his mannerisms suggested far more than words could have done.

Midge that night said, "I think we now have what we need to write our report."

"Indeed, Midge, we do. Why don't I write the draft? You can edit it. Tomorrow we can both travel home again. After our adventure with the Nazis, it would be a good idea for us to travel separately as we did while journeying here.

Harry and Midge spent their last married night in their Ethiopian lodgings. They departed the next day. Ten days later, they met the president's advisor by the Reflecting Pool where the Washington Monument was mirrored in the water. The man did not acknowledge either of the two adventurers. He did mutter something about there being three fewer Nazi goons in the world, At least that is what Midge thought she heard before he pocketed the report and got lost in the throngs of tourists.

"Well, Midge, it has been great working with you. I don't know if we'll ever see one another again."

"Harry," she replied as she stuck out her hand, "you sure know how to show a young lady a good time. Is it true you are the grandson of Annie Oakley?"

He shook her hand and said, "Yes, Midge, that part is true. As for being Harold Byrd, well …"

"It hardly matters, Harry … or whoever you are. I'm off this afternoon into the wild blue yonder. If we meet again, that's well and good. If not, it's been fun."

She spun on her heel and skipped off to catch a taxi for the airport.

The Wives Discuss ...

Alana Ballantyne

Long ago, in a town that thought itself much better than it was, lived a woman who did not have a husband.

Her name was Emily Hooper, and she was rapidly approaching the advanced age of thirty-two. Despite this, she had recently and inexplicably turned down a perfectly fine proposal from one Mr. James Crane, a local man who owned a large cannery in Columbus and was thus a very good match—especially for someone Emily's age. The resulting scandal had consumed the town; licking through every parlor and parish social hour like wildfire through kindling.

"I just don't know how her poor mother stands it." Mrs. Beasley sighed late one afternoon as she stirred her tea in her parlor. Mrs. Beasley was the kind of woman that other women liked to know. She was stately without being intimidating, her house was well kept, and she had raised four respectable children. On that afternoon, her Wednesday knitting circle surrounded her; all of them doing very little knitting as they considered the puzzle that was Emily Hooper.

"Three proposals!" Mrs. Ashland hissed, "The girl has turned down three proposals!"

"And they were all so decent." Mrs. Baker said sadly.

"Well, I should think so!" Mrs. Ashland exclaimed, "I knew she would never marry once she turned down my Henry. I told him …" she turned to Mrs. Beasley, "I told him that woman was no good for him. Too old, too educated. Once these modern girls go off to school, they get ideas, and she's just so … odd."

"Pretty, though." Mrs. Baker said sweetly, "Emily always was so pretty."

Mrs. Beasley nodded in agreement as Mrs. Marshall re-filled her teacup.

Mrs. Ashland sniffed, "She looks old now. And I never saw what all the fuss was about in the first place. She's fine to look at … too dark if you ask me … I just don't think swarthy girls like that are ladylike, too much sun, but she's nothing compared to my Rachel. Did you know that Arthur Beauchamp has been courting her? I expect Charles and I will be informed of an engagement in the spring—"

Mrs. Beasley and Mrs. Marshall exchanged a look. Rachel Ashland was very pretty, it was true, but she was no great beauty. Emily Hooper was a great beauty, even in her thirties. She had one of those faces that age seemed to enhance, rather than ruin.

"It's so strange," Mrs. Baker mused, cutting off Mrs. Ashland mid-ramble, "I'd think with the money gone, Emily would be eager to marry."

"Well, we don't know the money's gone." Mrs. Marshall said pointedly.

"How could it not be, with the banks as they are?" Mrs. Ashland exclaimed, "Why, my brother-in-law was nearly ruined! My sister had to come begging me for money for the children's school! It was terribly embarrassing for him, my sister told me he didn't speak to her for a week after Charles paid the bills for them."

"Why do men have to be so silly about these things?" Mrs. Baker said, shaking her head.

"Who knows?" Mrs. Marshall replied, rolling her eyes, "When I suggested we open the house to boarders—"

Mrs. Beasley looked up from her tea, shocked, "It's not that bad, is it?"

Mrs. Marshall grimaced, "I think it's worse than Thomas is letting on."

"Oh, why didn't you say something?" Mrs. Beasley reached out to clasp her friend's hand in her own.

Mrs. Marshall smiled tightly and shrugged, "There was nothing to say, really. You know the boys have both taken jobs … they were able to find work, thank the Lord. Katherine is still in school for now. I'm not sure how much more Thomas can do to keep the bank open. He's worked so hard—"

"You think the bank will close?" Mrs. Baker exclaimed. Mrs. Ashland set down her tea, fixing her hawkish eyes on Mrs. Marshall's now flushed countenance.

"I … I don't know." Mrs. Marshall stammered, looking down at her tea. "I try not to think about it. I read the papers, you know—"

"Oh, you really shouldn't," Mrs. Ashland said, "Charles says that Roosevelt is just fear-mongering. Reading won't help your nerves."

"I just don't see how things can continue on as they are." Mrs. Marshall continued as though Mrs. Ashland hadn't spoken, "Thomas spends all his time trying to keep the doors open over there. He's so short with me when he gets home. I hardly know what to do with myself anymore!" She sniffed, her eyes welling with tears.

Mrs. Beasley squeezed her friend's hand again and offered her a handkerchief, which Mrs. Marshall took gladly.

"Actually," Mrs. Marshall said, wiping her eyes, "I am a little glad Emily Hooper turned down Mr. Crane's proposal. Without her, I think things at the bank would be much worse than they are."

"Emily has been helping Thomas at the bank?" Mrs. Ashland asked sharply.

"Yes, yes. Something to do with her B.A, Thomas said. She's the only clerk he's had with a degree." Mrs. Marshall let out a small, watery chuckle, "I think she's there later than he is sometimes, if that's possible."

"I hadn't heard anything about Emily working at the bank." Mrs. Beasley frowned.

"No, I suppose you wouldn't have." Mrs. Marshall said, "I don't think Thomas would be comfortable if everyone knew just how much help she is. She really is a dear girl, Thomas just adores her."

"How is he paying her?" Mrs. Beasley asked.

Mrs. Marshall sighed, "I don't know that he is. That's why I don't think the money is gone. It can't be gone. Emily spends all of her time at the bank, and I haven't heard anything about Mrs. Hooper taking a job."

"Well I am sure poor, dear Mrs. Hooper is scandalized!" Mrs. Ashland exclaimed, "To think her daughter … her only child … turning down three proposals only to shutter up in a bank all day with a married man!"

"Mrs. Ashland!" Mrs. Beasley said warningly.

Mrs. Marshall looked stricken.

Mrs. Ashland held up her hands, "I am not saying anything is going on … I know Thomas better than that, but …" she looked around their semicircle, "Emily is that kind of girl. We all remember what happened—"

"Mrs. Ashland." Mrs. Beasley said again, in a tone that left no room for debate.

Mrs. Ashland pursed her lips but said nothing more.

"Ah-hem," Mrs. Baker cleared her throat nervously, "I've heard the most marvelous things about your azalea bushes, Mrs. Ashland."

The younger woman's blatant attempt to change the subject fell flat. The knitting circle lapsed into silence punctured only by the occasional sniffle from Mrs. Marshall. A few minutes passed in painful silence before Mrs. Marshall abruptly stood.

"I … I must be going now, I think," she said shakily, gathering her knitting things from around her chair.

"Oh, do stay dear," Mrs. Beasley implored, "I'll have Moll make us more tea."

"No, I really must be going." Mrs. Marshall said, clearly holding back tears, "I will see all of you on Sunday," and with a flurry of silk skirts, she was gone.

Mrs. Baker looked over at Mrs. Ashland, "You don't really think—"

"Well, it's possible!" Mrs. Ashland sniffed, "One can never be too careful with girls like Emily."

"Poor Mrs. Marshall …" Mrs. Baker said miserably, wringing her knitting between her hands.

"Really," Mrs. Beasley said, eyeing Mrs. Ashland reproachfully, "did you need to bring that old rumor up in front of her? Did you really need to imply—"

"It's a rumor only because no one was in the bedroom with them." Mrs. Ashland said as she pretended to continue knitting the stockings on her lap, "Everyone knows what happened. It's all anyone could talk about at the time. My goodness, the divorce particularly confirmed it!"

"Mrs. Andrews never said anything about an affair—"

"She didn't need to!" Mrs. Ashland said. She turned toward Mrs. Baker, "You went to school with her, did she show any … any signs at the time?"

"No, none at all. We had no idea. I had no idea …" Mrs. Baker stuttered, "We … we weren't close … but I wouldn't have thought it of her, but … but I guess—"

"We don't know—" Mrs. Beasley started.

"Of course, we know!" Mrs. Ashland exclaimed. "She was always the standoffish type, always reading. I told her mother, I told her that letting Emily do whatever she wanted would only encourage strange, immoral ideas. But you know how Emily's father was."

"I hardly ever saw that man at church." Mrs. Beasley mused, stirring her tea.

"He gave his daughter all kinds of ideas … let her run wild! And then she goes off to college and comes back worse than before! Who knows what they taught her there? Disgusting." Mrs. Ashland shook her head, "And when she came back she was all over that man, making eyes at him! To think, a married teacher! Her married teacher. She'd just graduated the year before after all."

"We don't know—" Mrs. Beasley tried to interject, but Mrs. Ashland waved her off.

"Of course, we do. Emily sweeps back into town that summer, college girl and all that." Mrs. Ashland scoffed, "She'd cut her hair, remember? I told Charles, I told him that she would be a problem and I. Was. Right!" she slammed her knitting needles down on the table in front of her.

"Mrs. Ashland," Mrs. Beasley said, setting down her own knitting, "We have absolutely no idea whether or not Emily was the cause of that divorce. Mrs. Andrews never hinted at anything of the kind. Neither of them did. Just because Emily was helping him with his research—"

"Why did she need to help him with anything at all?" Mrs. Ashland exclaimed, "What reason could she have possibly had?"

"He was writing a book of some kind ... wasn't he?" Mrs. Baker asked, scrunching her nose as she tried to remember, "Wasn't it something about ... about frogs or toads?"

"It was an anthology of all the species of frogs that live in the Ohio riverbed, I believe." Mrs. Beasley said, smoothing her hair, "His mother was quite proud of his work. I spoke with her at length about it shortly before she passed last autumn."

"Useless." Mrs. Ashland muttered as she took a sip of her tea.

"It was actually quite interesting." Mrs. Beasley countered, picking up her knitting once more, "It was published, you know."

"Yes, but not until after all that business with the war." Mrs. Ashland said, "I heard that he never would have been published if he hadn't lost his legs."

Mrs. Baker looked horrified, "What a terrible thing to say!"

"And who could have possibly told you that?" snapped Mrs. Beasley, clearly at the end of her patience.

"I don't remember, I just remember that it was said at the time." Mrs. Ashland said primly, though she flushed a little as she did so.

"I don't put stock in vicious rumors like that." Mrs. Beasley said, sitting up straighter in her chair, "I thought the boy was quite talented. He made the whole frog business seem interesting, and you know I am not one for that kind of reading."

"Boy." Mrs. Baker said, seeming to turn the word over in her head, "It's so funny to hear you call him a boy. I always thought of him as so old back in school."

Mrs. Beasley laughed, "I suppose he would have seemed old to you. After all, you were only a girl when the Andrews moved into town. They were quite the couple when they came here. He'd just finished his studies in Chicago, I believe."

"Why would they want to move all the way out here?" Mrs. Baker asked.

"The former Mrs. Andrews was not partial to city life, apparently," said Mrs. Beasley, "It is my understanding that she was from somewhere outside of Cleveland originally. I think they decided that they wanted a taste of rural living."

"For all the good it did them," Mrs. Ashland muttered.

Mrs. Beasley sighed in irritation, "Just because they got divorced after Emily began helping him with his book does not mean there was an affair!"

Mrs. Ashland narrowed her eyes, "It doesn't mean there wasn't either."

"I'm out of tea," Mrs. Baker interjected, clearly trying to avoid the brewing argument.

"I'll ring Moll," Mrs. Beasley said, reaching for a small bell on the parlor table. Once she rang it, a pale girl in a smart uniform appeared in the doorway to the kitchen.

"Yes, Mrs. Beasley?"

"Get Mrs. Baker some more tea, dear."

With a quick bow, Moll vanished back into the kitchen.

The women knit in silence for a few minutes, each considering the half-forgotten scandal from over a decade prior. After a few minutes of quiet, Mrs. Ashland could contain herself no longer.

"It is odd," she said, glancing sideways at her companions.

Mrs. Bealey sighed and took the bait with an air of resignation, "What is odd?"

"How Emily never, you know," Mrs. Ashland lowered her voice to a loud whisper, as though Moll had her ear pressed up against the kitchen door, "carried on with Mr. Andrews after the divorce."

"It lends credence to the idea that there was no affair, to begin with." Mrs. Beasley said primly.

Mrs. Baker hummed in tepid agreement.

"I heard that when he came back from the War he asked to court her and she turned him down." Mrs. Ashland said, "Rather cold, if you ask me. After all, he gave up his marriage for her."

"Allegedly," Mrs. Beasley interjected.

"Well, that at least makes sense. He … he was different when he came back." Mrs. Baker said, clearly trying to be delicate.

"I never got the sense that Emily was the type to care about things like that, especially if we accept that she had already carried on such a long affair with him prior to that," Mrs. Beasley said.

"I don't think she had any such affair ma'am."

All three women looked up from their knitting at the sudden interruption. Moll stood framed in the doorway, twisting her apron between her slender hands.

Mrs. Beasley recovered first, "Moll, what makes you say that?"

"Emily ain't that kind of girl, ma'am. And pardon me for saying so, but Mr. Nicolas and Mrs. Rachel never did get along that well. Not for a very long time. They was fighting long before Miss Emily was ever in Mr. Nicolas' class."

"How do you know that?" demanded Mrs. Ashland, "Were you spying on them?"

"N-no, ma'am." Moll stuttered, "I just … their serving girl, Oppie? She were a friend of my mother's. I would hear them talk about it sometimes, that's all."

"Servant's gossip," Mrs. Ashland said dismissively, "What would they know of it?"

"Apparently a great deal more than us," Mrs. Beasley said pointedly, "Thank you, Moll. The tea?"

Moll nodded from the doorway, "Yes, Mrs. Beasley."

She returned from the kitchen with the teapot and refilled each woman's cup with an experienced flourish before retreating once more into the backrooms of the house. Mrs. Ashland watched her leave with a cold expression.

When she was sure the girl had returned to her duties, Mrs. Ashland glanced at Mrs. Beasley as she took a sip of her tea, "You really should discipline your help better, my dear. I would never stand for a common girl like that daring to intrude on a conversation that had nothing to do with her. Charles would go mad if any of our servants even thought to try it."

"Moll is a sweet girl." Mrs. Beasley said, "I won't punish her for standing up for someone else."

"Standing up for? We were hardly disparaging Emily." Mrs. Ashland scoffed.

"Weren't we?" Mrs. Baker asked, determinedly not making eye contact with Mrs. Ashland.

"We weren't." Mrs. Ashland said firmly, as though that put and end to it, "The affairs of the town are always of great public importance, especially where the morality of its citizens is concerned. It's only right that we discuss it."

"I wasn't aware that you had taken up the pulpit, Mrs. Ashland." Mrs. Beasley said mildly, "And I hardly see how discussing events long in the past have moral significance now."

Mrs. Ashland shook her head, "Those events have directly contributed to the predicament that we now find ourselves facing!"

"And what predicament is that?" Mrs. Beasley asked.

"Why Emily Hooper's rejection of Mr. Crane of course!" exclaimed Mrs. Ashland.

"I hardly see how that is a predicament for us," said Mrs. Beasley, "Emily is the one who will reap the consequences of her decision."

Mrs. Ashland crossed her arms, "Be that as it may, there is something … immoral about a girl with her reputation remaining unmarried for so long. It damages the atmosphere of the community."

Mrs. Beasley rolled her eyes but said nothing.

"I'm sure she had a good reason." Mrs. Baker said, "Emily was always very smart—"

"She can't be that smart, she turned down one of the most eligible bachelors between here and Columbus!" said Mrs. Ashland.

"That was … foolish of her," Mrs. Beasley agreed, setting her knitting aside and taking a sip of her tea. "That will most likely be the last proposal she'll ever receive."

"There was no reason to turn Mr. Crane down." Mrs. Ashland huffed.

"Perhaps she didn't love him." Mrs. Baker suggested quietly.

"Love him? Ha!" barked Mrs. Ashfield, "If you were as old as she is and still single, do you think you could afford luxurious considerations like love?"

"Shouldn't a husband love his wife?" Mrs. Baker asked, her cheeks flushing slightly, "And shouldn't a woman marry someone she loves?"

"I suppose so," Mrs. Beasley said, absentmindedly returning to her knitting, "though love shouldn't be the only consideration. What will Emily do when her mother passes on? Who will take care of her then?"

Mrs. Baker thought for a moment, "Maybe Emily will care for herself. She seems to have done alright so far, whether the money is gone or not. She always seemed like the kind of girl that could handle herself, even when we were in school."

"Perhaps," said Mrs. Beasley, though she frowned as she took another sip of tea.

"Charles doesn't think she should be allowed to be about town," Mrs. Ashland said. "He thinks it will give the other young girls ideas."

"Ideas?" Mrs. Baker asked.

"Yes. Going off to school and the like," Mrs. Ashland said.

Mrs. Baker frowned, "I think I want my daughter to try for her B.A."

"Whatever for?" Mrs. Ashland asked, "Olivia is a fine girl. You don't want her to go off to college and come back with ideas, would you? You wouldn't want her to remain a spinster, like Emily, would you?"

"Of course not." Mrs. Baker flushed, "Only ... I do like the way Emily speaks sometimes. She sounds so ... worldly."

"I'll bet she's worldly," Mrs. Ashland said under her breath. "For all her education she has nothing. No family besides her mother. God bless her. No suitors, no close friends. She is alone with her books, and apparently, Mr. Marshall."

Mrs. Beasley shot her a look.

Mrs. Baker frowned, "She seems … happy. Even without all those things you listed. Every time I see her she's smiling."

"I'm sure it's a façade," Mrs. Ashland said assuredly. "No woman can be happy alone. It is simply not the way of things."

"Do you ever think about what you might have been if you hadn't gotten married?" asked Mrs. Baker suddenly.

Mrs. Ashland tutted, "I've never thought about it. Why would I?"

"I don't know," said Mrs. Baker, shrugging, "I've thought about it, that's all. I guess I was just wondering if it was … common."

"Common? Certainly not." Mrs. Ashland huffed, resuming her knitting.

"I've thought about it," Mrs. Beasley said quietly. Mrs. Ashland and Mrs. Baker turned to look at her.

"Mrs. *Beasley!*" Mrs. Ashland gasped.

"I didn't want to marry Don when he first asked me." Mrs. Beasley continued, "I thought I would finish school, maybe go off to college, like Emily did. Only, in those days, no one went off to college, not even the boys. I think my father was the only college man in town then."

"What did he do?" asked Mrs. Baker.

"He was a doctor," said Mrs. Beasley, "He was a wonderful doctor. He was very attentive, kind, generous with his time. When I was a little girl, I thought I would grow up and become a doctor just like him."

Mrs. Baker frowned, "Why didn't you?"

"What a question!" Mrs. Ashland scoffed, "She grew up! She got her priorities straight. Don Beasley was an excellent match for her. His family is well-connected, he was wealthy—"

"I gave up," Mrs. Beasley said.

Her companions stared at her in shock, their knitting laying forgotten on their laps.

"I thought that I couldn't ... shouldn't ... want for more than I had," Mrs. Beasley sighed. "I felt that I would, oh I don't know ... let people down if I refused to marry. My parents, my friends, Don ..." she trailed off.

"The world is not made for women with dreams," said Mrs. Baker.

"What a thing to say!" Mrs. Ashland exclaimed, setting her knitting down on the table, "My dear Mrs. Beasley, you can't mean that you regret marrying your husband!"

Mrs. Beasley did not reply for quite some time. When she finally spoke, it was with the air of one who had lost a dear friend, "I don't regret marrying Don. Or having my children. It is more that I regret the opportunity that was denied, in some ways, to me."

"I wish I had more time to myself, sometimes." Mrs. Baker admitted, "I … I think about what it would be like to be like Emily. Just sometimes." She looked around at her companions, "I mean she has all the time she wants to read, or write, or help at the bank. She has no children to care for, no husband to cook for. She has her own career—"

"And what on earth would you need a career for?" Mrs. Ashland demanded.

Mrs. Baker shrugged, "I don't know that I would. I've never had one before. It's just that some days I wish that I could try it. Just once. It might be nice to have my own money, my own time, my own home."

"Maybe," Mrs. Beasley said contemplatively, "that is why Emily is happy as she is. Alone."

And after that, there seemed to be nothing more to say. Mrs. Ashland left first, wearing the stoney expression of one who had witnessed something unspeakable and could not wait to be rid of it. Mrs. Baker lingered longer, making small talk with Mrs. Beasley until the afternoon shadows had lengthened to the point that they could no longer be ignored.

Mrs. Beasley watched her younger friend depart from her doorway. Somehow, Mrs. Beasley knew that they would never discuss their desires again. What had passed between them had been honest, but unwise.

Mrs. Beasley closed her door and returned to her parlor. She allowed herself, just for a moment, to remember when there had been no Mrs. Beasley, with her duties and family, only Catherine, with her hopes and dreams.

She wept.

Contributors

Alana Ballantyne is a freelance journalist and short story writer. Her work has previously appeared in Ink & Voices and Chaleur Magazine.

She is currently pursuing her J.D at Michigan State University.

Joanna Bair has a BA in English and Theatre. With an extensive background in theatre and dance she's written and produced plays in the U.S. and Malta.

Her short stories have been published in Splickety, Keys for Kids, and Zimbell House's anthology Trail's End.

The inspiration for this story came from a visit to the massive villa in Bagheria her great grandfather left during the first World War to avoid the draft and a newspaper article about the mafia.

E. W. Farnsworth

E. W. Farnsworth is widely published online and in print. Many of his stories are fictions based on fact.

For additional information about the author, please see:

http://www.ewfarnsworth.com.

Matt McGee

Matt McGee writes short fiction in the Los Angeles area, where he developed his affection for old radio shows as they were broadcast on local station KNX1070 AM. This 'theatre of the mind' has been his playground ever since and sees him off to sleep every night.

His work has twice appeared in Zimbell House's anthologies, *On a Dark & Snowy Night* and *Why?*

In 2018, his stories 'A Day in the Life of a Favor Saver' and 'Schneider's Last Stand' have appeared in Grey Wolfe Press' *Legends* anthology, 'The Flaming Tadpoles' will appear in the UK-based *Painted Words* anthology in July, 2018, and his first romance novel, *Wildwood Mountain,* was released June 19, 2018.

When not typing he drives around in a vintage Mazda and plays goalie in local hockey leagues.

Matt received technical help on this story from Jeanette Barard, at the American Radio Archives in Thousand Oaks, California. He feels it's an incredible resource for anyone wishing to research any era of media, particularly radio.

Their website can be reached via:

http://www.americanradioarchives.com/

Similar Anthologies from Zimbell House

The Mysteries of Suspense

Pagan

Tales from the Grave

Curse of the Tomb Seekers

Travelers

Dark Monsters

On a Dark and Snowy Night

The Key

Veil of Secrets

The Lost Door

Nocturnal Natures

The Neighbors

Why? A Collection of Mysterious Tales

River Tales

After Effect

Ghost Stories

No Trace

Midnight Rising

Coming Soon from Zimbell House

Shifting

November Falls

Join our mailing list to receive updates on new
releases, discounts, bonus content, and other
great books from

Or visit us online to sign up:

http://www.ZimbellHousePublishing.com

A Note from the Publisher

How to Thank a Contributor

Dear Reader,

Everyone at Zimbell House Publishing would like to thank you for reading *Not Anyone's Wife*. If you would like to thank a particular contributor, the best way is to leave a review for them. You may do so by leaving one on our Goodreads page, under the *Not Anyone's Wife* title, by using the link below:

http://www.goodreads.com/ZimbellHousePublishing

and be sure to mention the contributor directly.

Why should you leave a review? Reviews help budding authors build their credibility in the book industry. By posting a review on Goodreads, you help other readers find new authors they may wish to follow, and you never know, your review may end up on an author's website one day.

Friend us on Goodreads:
https://www.goodreads.com/ZimbellHousePublishing

Follow us on Twitter:
http://twitter.com/ZimbellHousePub

9 781947 210639